SALT PEANUTS

SALT PEANUTS

A Novel by

Brian David

Library of Congress Control Number: 2018903229
ISBN: Hardcover 978-1-9845-1535-3
Softcover 978-1-9845-1537-7
eBook 978-1-9845-1536-0

Print information available on the last page.

Rev. date: 05/22/2018

To order additional copies of this book, contact:
Xlibris
1-888-795-4274
www.Xlibris.com
Orders@Xlibris.com
774286

For Cookie, Alison and Sam

note from the author

I practiced law for forty years, the last thirty of which specialized in the representation of professional baseball players. My introduction into the baseball business came in the early 1980s when I represented Hall of Famer Orlando Cepeda well after his playing career. At the time I met him, unfortunately, he was serving time in a federal penitentiary in Eglin, Florida, following a criminal conviction for importing marijuana into Puerto Rico. I represented Orlando in two proceedings: (1) motion for reduction of sentence in the United States District Court in San Juan, Puerto Rico, and (2) proceedings before the U.S. Parole Board in Eglin, Florida. We were able to achieve a favorable result for Orlando, and the following winter, through him, I met ballplayers playing winter baseball in Puerto Rico.

During the 1980s, as part of my law practice, I represented such players as Lee Smith, Willie Hernandez, Thad Bosley, Lenny Randle, Mike Perez, Wade Boggs, and Marty Barrett. In 1985 I presented an arbitration case on behalf of Wade Boggs (another current Hall of Famer) that resulted in the first ever $1 million arbitration award to a player. Later I joined the baseball agency

Speakers of Sport, Inc. (which we subsequently sold to SFX Baseball Group in 2000). I remained at SFX in the capacity of legal counsel until my departure in 2012. Over the years I was involved in the filing of hundreds of arbitration cases and participated in the presentation of approximately twenty such hearings. Also during that time I was extensively involved in the negotiation and drafting of numerous multimillion-dollar contracts, including those for David Ortiz, Pedro Martinez, Alfonso Soriano, Miguel Tejada, Vladmir Guerrero, Mariano Rivera, Miguel Cabrera, and Jim Thome.

When I left SFX in 2012, a few people suggested I write a book about my experience as an agent or about how to become an agent, but I had no interest in doing that. I did, however, have an interest in trying to write a novel drawing from some of my experiences. Many of the players I dealt with in my career were of Hispanic descent. Most fans do not grasp the difficulty associated with making the adjustment to life in America coming from a foreign land to becoming a professional baseball player in America. I found it particularly interesting to contemplate what a Cuban defector must go through on and off the baseball field. Not only do they have to go through the difficult adjustment of language and culture, but also they carry the added burden of leaving their homeland forever where they are branded as traitors. I felt that could form the basis for an informative, entertaining story and was the inspiration for writing this book.

My goals here are to communicate my passion for the great game of baseball into a story which, hopefully, enlightens readers about what Latin players experience in their attempted rise to the major leagues and more specifically, what a Cuban defector experiences after he leaves behind his family and homeland. Moreover, I hope to tell this story in the historical context of the complex and controversial history between the United States and Cuba.

PROLOGUE

Baseball has been played in Cuba since the 1860s. The "Sugar Leagues," were started by those working in the sugar plantations as a way of passing the time while they waited for the cane to grow. The pace of the game and the hot Carribean days suited the Cuban people and once baseball fever hit the island, it never left. The country's passion for the game led to the development of the Cuban National Team, which became a significant source of pride to the island and consistently one of the strongest teams in the world.

In the years prior to 1959, when Fidel Castro overthrew dictator Fulgencio Batista, Cuba produced more major league baseball players than any other Latin American country. That all changed after the revolution as Castro enforced his anti-capitalist philosophy. He felt that Cuban ballplayers should compete for his country and his people only. For the next thirty years, virtually no Cuban players were able to come to America, let alone break into major leagues. That began to change in 1991 when pitcher Rene Arocha walked off an airplane that made an emergency stop in Miami and didn't return home. He signed a contract with the St. Louis Cardinals. A few years later, Rolando Arrojo, Livian Hernandez, and Orlando Hernandez all defected, thus beginning the exodus.

However, players just can't leave Cuba. Simply inquiring about going to the United States can result in being labeled as a subversive and an enemy of the state. Those looking to escape the Castro regime have to be illegally smuggled out of the country. This has become a big and very dangerous business, which is why leaving Cuba is a risky proposition. Latin American stars from the Dominican Republic, Puerto Rico, Venezuela, Panama, and Mexico are treated like heroes when they return to their homelands, but the Cuban government views their defectors as disloyal traitors who are not allowed back into their country. Many defectors are unable to see their families ever again.

The United States has passed laws and developed policies in an attempt to provide a path to asylum and residency, but traveling the ninety miles across the dangerous waters of the Florida Straits can be deadly, especially for ill-equipped vessels attempting to make the illegal journey. Ever since the Soviet Union dissolved in 1989 and Cuba stopped receiving subsidies from them, the number of attempted defections to America has steadily risen. Amnesty International estimates that over 100,000 people lost their lives trying to escape Cuba by water.

If getting to the United States wasn't difficult enough for Cuban players, it's only half the battle. Not every player receives multimillion-dollar contracts and becomes a star. Most receive only minor league contracts and never make it to the big leagues. Some of the biggest problems Cuban players encounter occur off the field. How these players adjust to American culture once they arrive proves to be the more difficult challenge.

Pinar del Rio, Cuba, 2004

CHAPTER 1

Standing inside the on-deck circle, a line of sweat rolled down the cheek of twenty-four-year-old Miguel Mijares as he studied the rookie reliever on the mound.

Six feet two inches and two hundred pounds, Miguel was the brightest star the Cuban League had seen in a decade. The numbers he put up last year for the Pinar del Rio Vegueros not only made him an All-Star, but some were calling him the best center fielder ever produced by the island. Only nobody called him Miguel anymore. Once he made a name for himself as a twelve-year-old ball player in the back lots of Pinar del Rio, people started calling him Mimi. The name stuck.

It was another ninety-degree Saturday afternoon. There was one out in the bottom of the ninth inning. The Vegueros were down 3-2 to the Cienfuegos Elefantes, but with a runner on second, the winning run was at the plate. From the on-deck circle, Mimi watched his teammate, first baseman Juan Perez, swing and miss at the second straight pitch. The catcher signaled for time and jogged out to the mound. Mimi couldn't help but smile as he saw the pitcher glance in his direction. He knew they weren't talking about Juan. They were talking about how to pitch to him.

Mimi winked back at the pitcher. He'd only faced the young southpaw once that afternoon. He grounded out but saw all he needed to understand this kid's tendencies.

Mimi took one more practice swing and looked out into the crowd. A couple hundred fans packed around the rusted wire fence surrounding this scorched patch of earth that passed for a baseball field. Nobody dared to sit in the bleachers after they collapsed years earlier, but nobody cared. This tobacco farming town less than fifty miles outside of Havana lived for baseball. The kids played year round, and those not lucky enough to play for their province made sure to watch every game. These were their people out on the field representing them.

What nobody else in the stadium knew that afternoon was that this would be Mimi's last game in Cuba. With the help of his father, he had been making arrangements to defect to the United States where he could have a better life and a shot at playing major league baseball. The escape had been carefully planned, and a close friend of his father had been paid to take Mimi to the Florida Keys in the middle of the night. If he were caught, it could mean house arrest or even prison time, but it was well worth the risk. As a little kid, he dreamed of stepping into the batter's box at Yankee Stadium. That dream was closer to becoming a reality for Mimi. Like any competitor, he wanted the chance to play against the best and the best played in America. He dreamed of taking the field alongside Derek Jeter on Opening Day and squaring off against

Pedro Martinez with the game on the line—not playing games in the Cuban League for thirty dollars a month.

"Two more outs and we go home. Mimi's got nothing today," shouted Cienfuegos third baseman Alejandro Castillo in Spanish. This snapped Mimi out of his trance. Alejandro had been taunting Mimi the entire game and knew exactly how to get under his skin.

Mimi was close to losing his cool, partly because Alejandro was right. He was 0 for 3 today and hadn't been able to make solid contact. His mind was elsewhere and his head wasn't in the game like it normally was—a wrong he wanted to right with this next at-bat. Like any natural-born hitter, he loved the spotlight. He loved the chance to be the hero. He loved being able to change the outcome of the game with one swing of the bat. Sure, he felt the pressure, but that's what made the game fun for him.

When play resumed, the pitcher threw a slider toward home plate that Juan popped up. The right fielder easily caught it for the second out of the ninth inning. The crowd began cheering louder than they had all day as Mimi stepped into the batter's box. Down one run with two outs in the bottom of the ninth, it was now up to Mimi. With a runner on second, a double might be all the Vegueros needed to send the game into extra innings, but Mimi's mind wasn't on tying the game. His mind was on winning, and with one pitch if possible. Mimi dug into the batter's box. He held the bat high—one of his trademark techniques. As soon as he stared down the pitcher, he could tell the young rookie was psyched out. He had him.

The pitcher wound up and let fly a fastball with everything he had, but he didn't have control and missed the strike zone by six inches. The second pitch was high and outside. The third was in the dirt. The count was now 3-0. The rookie wasn't trying to walk Mimi. This kid was trying to challenge him with fastballs and prove that he could strike out the best. Luckily for the pitcher, the umpire called for time as a fight in the crowd spilled out onto the field. The police quickly pulled the two drunken fans apart and escorted them away.

Time resumed and Mimi dug back in. As soon as the ball left the pitcher's hand, Mimi saw that it was going to be high and outside. This would be ball four, but the last thing Mimi wanted to do during his final at-bat in Cuba was walk. He did what no fundamentally sound baseball player would ever consider in that situation, especially since he represented the winning run—he stretched and swung at a pitch way out of the strike zone and sliced a line drive right down the first baseline.

Mimi was halfway to first when he saw the ball land in fair territory. As he rounded the base, he already had third on his mind. He didn't look over his shoulder at the right fielder, and he didn't look at his third base coach. He didn't see his teammate cross home and tie the game, nor was he thinking that he'd be the goat if thrown out trying to stretch a double into a triple. He just touched the old stuffed flour sack being used as second base and sprinted as hard as he could toward third. If there were any major league scouts in the crowd, they wouldn't believe the speed they were witnessing. They probably never saw anybody kick it into high gear like Mimi as he slid into third a half-second ahead of the throw.

Before the umpire could signal safe, Mimi saw the ball skid out of Alejandro's glove. Mimi didn't think twice before popping up and heading for home. If Alejandro didn't hesitate, he could have easily sprinted ten feet to get the ball and throw Mimi out at home, but he did hesitate. That's what separated Mimi from other players. It wasn't just about talent; it was about instinct. He didn't worry about failing. He gave it everything he had on every play and he didn't have to try—it came naturally. It was only a brief second before Alejandro realized Mimi was attempting what very few base runners would have had the confidence to even think about, but that extra second was all Mimi needed. Alejandro panicked and bobbled the ball. Mimi crossed home after a picture-perfect headfirst slide before the throw was even made.

The rest of the team raced out of the dugout and rushed Mimi. Even the teammates he had played with for years were still in awe of what they witnessed him do on a daily basis. The fans were on their feet! This was why people came from miles around to watch Mimi play. It seemed like he would do something extraordinary every game. It might be an amazing catch in the outfield. It might be one of his laser-like throws from center field to nail an unsuspecting base runner, or it might be seeing the way the ball shot off his bat whenever he made contact. The energy on the field and in the crowd was electric, but to the fans it was just another Saturday. This was Cuban baseball.

On his way back to the dugout, all Mimi could think about was grabbing his bat and glove so he could get off the field as quickly as possible. This was the other side to the Cuban All-Star. As vibrant a player as he was on the field, off the field he was introverted and shy. He always wanted to be the best, but once he became the best, he realized that he wasn't equipped to handle the attention off the field. A part of him felt guilty that he could still play the game he loved while many of his friends didn't make it this far and were stuck working at the mill or out in the cane fields. His friends now treated him like a star, but he missed their old dynamic when they could laugh and joke with each other as equals. Now it felt like they were competing for his attention, and sometimes his approval. As Mimi's celebrity grew, the more he found himself gravitating toward his family because they had always treated him the same. To them he wasn't Mimi, he was Miguel.

When the chaos outside the dugout died down, Mimi made his break for it. He knew this path behind the field particularly well because it was the quickest way for him to cut to the makeshift locker room without being mobbed by the adoring, and often drunken, fans. He always made sure to smile and be grateful—that's something his father taught him at a very young age. On the field he could showboat as long as he could back up his talk, but when he taunted opposing fans after winning a youth game, his dad dragged him away from the field by his ear. His father always talked about learning humility from "Jesus de la Pelota, the Supreme God of baseball."

Mimi was in the clear, ten feet away from the locker room door, when he heard a young voice call out, "Mimi! *Aqui*!" He turned to see a young boy standing with his working-class father. The boy, who was wearing a T-shirt that he clearly made himself to look like Mimi's game jersey, held out his glove and a pen for

Mimi to sign. Mimi had a soft spot for the kids. The adults were trying to get a reaction out of him, but the kids were genuine. They loved the game. He remembered when he was a young boy coming to this same field hoping to catch a glimpse of players like Danielo Baez, Yunesky Maya, and Luis Casanova after the game. Sometimes they breezed right by him, but when they did stop, it would make his day. That's why Mimi always stopped.

He walked over to the boy, but instead of signing the boy's glove, Mimi offered up his own glove. Father and son were both shocked, but Mimi disappeared into the locker room before either of them had a chance to thank him.

Once inside, Mimi sat on his stool and watched his teammates celebrate. He'd miss moments like this but tried to remind himself of the opportunity that waited for him in America. However, his desire to defect wasn't only about baseball. Mimi never hesitated to talk about how the Cuban people were robbed of basic human rights under Fidel. The government owned everyone's property and, even worse, everyone's soul. They provided education and medical care, but in return took away freedom of speech and freedom of expression. Before the game today, he and his teammates were forced to attend a meeting for the purpose of listening to political speeches by Fidel's confidants. Why? Mimi thought it was absurd. They were about to play a game. Just leave us alone. But then again, Castro would regularly schedule exhibition games with countries as part of a trade negotiation. In spite of baseball's popularity and significance, most Cuban ballplayers had to find part-time work in the off-season. There were no autograph shows or endorsement deals. Even stars like Mimi had to fight to survive just like everyone else. They all heard stories about the big-money contracts being handed out like candy to players in America, but Mimi couldn't wrap his head around that kind of wealth. A huge contract would be nice, but what would he buy? It was never about the money. All he wanted was to make enough to provide a better life for his family.

Once he was dressed, Mimi grabbed the small bag he packed to take with him to America and slipped out the door before anybody realized he was gone.

CHAPTER 2

Mimi walked into the dirt parking lot behind the field and spotted his father's rusted Datsun pickup idling in the corner.

Osvaldo, or Ozzie as everyone called him, worked Saturday afternoons at the sugarcane processing company. He could rarely see his son's games in person, but he made sure to listen on the radio. On his way home, Ozzie would always swing by the field to pick up Mimi and drive him back to the family house for dinner. Mimi's mother, Anna, loved to cook and spent all day preparing the Saturday meal. It had become a tradition, and it allowed Mimi to spend time with his younger brother, Manny, whom he didn't see much since he moved out of the family house and into his own apartment a few years earlier. After dinner, Ozzie would always drive Mimi home and try to prepare him for his next game. Tonight was different. They'd be making the four-hour drive to the shore to meet Ozzie's friend, Gato. He owned a boat and would secretly use it to bring those looking to defect to Florida.

Mimi tossed his bag in the back of the truck and climbed into the passenger seat. Before he even closed the door, his dad started talking about the game.

"*Manos*."

"*Como*?"

"At the plate. Were you dropping your hands again?"

Ozzie loved to talk about the game on the drive to the house, but today the game was the last thing on Mimi's mind.

"And why swing at ball four in a 3-0 count?" added his father.

"I wasn't going to let him walk me."

After a long silence, Ozzie asked, "How much were they paying Juan to throw that game?"

A couple of years ago, the Pinar del Rio Club found itself in the middle of a scandal when four players were suspected of accepting bribe money. During the 1970s and 1980s, Cuban authorities permanently banned several players and coaches for accepting bribes to fix games. It was less of a problem now, but players needed money so every so often some were paid to throw games by local bookies. Mimi knew that Juan had recently fallen on tough times, but it was heartbreaking to think that he might have accepted money.

"Juan? No," said Mimi, but he could see that his father was right.

"He popped out four times and then made that error in the third."

It's no surprise that Ozzie sniffed it out—even while listening to the radio. In another life, Ozzie could have been a great scout. He played ball as a kid, and he was good, but he put all of that behind him and went to work at the mill at the age of eighteen when Anna became pregnant. Mimi knew his father hated his job and didn't make much money, but he never once heard Ozzie complain, even though he had every right to. This was another reason why Mimi wanted out of Cuba. He often wondered how much longer he could play here before he considered accepting money to help his family.

"*Lo siento.*" Mimi's head was elsewhere. "I can't talk about the game right now."

Ozzie let it go. He ruffled Mimi's hair and turned his attention to the road. They drove in silence for a mile before Mimi finally opened up about what was really on his mind.

"Have you seen Gato's boat? How well does he know the waters?"

Mimi was now obsessing over all the things that could go wrong on the trip. He remembered seeing Gato at the cane factory when he would go there with his father as a boy. The man certainly didn't appear to be the toughest or most capable of sailors. What happened if something went wrong? Everyone in Cuba was well aware of the "wet foot, dry foot" policy that stated if a Cuban defector made it to U.S. soil, he would be allowed to stay, but if found in the water between the two nations, he would be sent back to Cuba and face possible imprisonment.

"You'll be in God's hands. Just focus on the things that you can control," said Ozzie, who remained calm and cracked a smile. Ozzie never had to say much, but he had a way of making Mimi feel better and could put a dire problem into perspective.

The truck pulled down a street with old dilapidated homes and overgrown grass. The three young children playing in the yard of one home waved to Mimi as they drove by. The truck came to a stop in front of the blue one-story home at the end of the road where Mimi grew up. It was in bad shape. Ozzie was able to provide the basics for his family, but food shortages were commonplace. Just last month Anna had to stretch a dozen plantains into a week's worth of meals. The poverty and sacrifices made by the Cuban people wasn't lost on Mimi who spent the past couple of years educating himself on Cuban history.

As Mimi reached for the door handle, his father put an arm on his shoulder.

"The hardest part of your journey will be right now."

Mimi was forced to keep the plan a secret from his mother and brother for their own safety. He didn't want his mother worrying, but he knew that slipping away in the middle of the night without properly saying goodbye would destroy her.

Ozzie added, "Say goodbye in your own way. I'll tell Mama when the time is right."

Mimi left his bag in the back of the truck to avoid raising any suspicion and followed Ozzie up to the house. He could smell his mother's homemade *boliche* as soon as he walked in the front door. When he saw Anna standing over the stove, he almost broke down, but instead, wrapped her in a hug and didn't let go.

"Dinner will be ready soon," said Anna.

He pulled away before she could sense that anything was wrong. When he dipped a piece of bread into the sauce simmering on the stove, she playfully pushed him away.

"Miguel! *Escucha*!"

"Is Manny in his room?"

"*Por supuesto*."

Ozzie was already settled into his lounge chair as Mimi walked through the living room and down the narrow hall that led to the two other rooms in the house—his parents' bedroom and the room he once shared with his younger brother before moving out. Now it was Manny's room. Mimi could see the light on under the door when he knocked.

"You in there? It's me."

"*Si*, come in," came the voice from inside.

Every time Mimi stepped inside his old room, it felt like he was taking a trip back to his childhood. The Yankees pennant and all the old baseball posters still hung on the wall, though now they were faded after years of being in the sun.

Manny sat on the bed. He was a chubby fifteen-year-old who wasn't half the athlete Mimi was, but loved the game of baseball just as much. Manny would rather watch than play. By his side was a book he could barely understand, but was unable to put down: *The Bronx Zoo* by Sparky Lyle. It was the story of the 1978 New York Yankees told by the pitcher himself. As a boy, Mimi carried this book everywhere and poured over the pages trying to teach himself English, but with little success. When Mimi moved out, he gave the book to Manny, who now cherished it like the Bible.

"Did they make it to the World Series yet?" asked Mimi as he flipped through the pages, searching for the spot where they left off.

"No, not yet. I marked the page."

What's funny was that Mimi didn't actually read the book to his brother. His English wasn't nearly as strong as he liked, and reading a book like that was far beyond his comprehension level, so he recited the story from memory. This was the same story his dad told him as a boy so it changed over the years, and with each retelling. Mimi didn't need to open the book. He could easily rattle off the next part of the story, but something about going through the book page by page helped bring the story to life. The smell of the pages. The glossy pictures. It all reminded him of a time when he fell in love with the game. Mimi was ten minutes into telling Manny about the Yankee's wild playoff run when Anna called the family to dinner.

The day was stressful, but Mimi felt at home once he sat down at the table. For an hour, he forgot about that day's game and all the different things that could go wrong on the journey that night. He enjoyed this time with his family. It wasn't until he was washing dishes with Manny, something they did after every dinner together for as long as he could remember when reality began to set in.

"After your game next Saturday, we're having a fiesta for Mama. It's supposed to be a surprise, but you know she's going to find out," said Manny.

Mimi's heart sank realizing he wouldn't be there. He felt like he was going to be sick.

"I'm sorry. Can you finish up? I need to get some air."

Mimi didn't wait for a response. He left Manny with a sink full of dishes and slipped out the back door. He walked through the old neighborhood and stopped to watch a group of kids playing baseball in the alley under a dim streetlight.

Mimi remembered playing here when he was young. This was where Ozzie and his ballplayer friends taught him to play the game. Ten years earlier, this was also where Mimi first told his father about his desire to play in America. After a long day of batting practice, they were sharing a Coke under the palm tree that also served as the right field foul pole when Mimi spoke about playing for the New York Yankees. Ozzie knew the danger and warned his son to keep this particular dream to himself. Ozzie's initial response was one of sadness and fear. He also knew Mimi very well, and knew that his son wouldn't stop until he achieved his dream so they worked together to make it happen. Ozzie saw it through and held up his end of the bargain. He always did. What Mimi found funny was now that the opportunity was here, all he could think about were the things he would miss when he was gone and how he took so much for granted.

Mimi must have watched the kids play for an hour before he turned and walked back home. As he approached the house, he saw his father sitting on the front steps, smoking a cigarette as he waited for him to return.

"Are you ready?" asked Ozzie as he got to his feet and dug his keys out of his pocket.

Mimi nodded and walked inside. He poked his head into Manny's room, but his brother was already asleep. He closed the door softly and turned around to find Anna standing there waiting with a plate of food for him to take back to his apartment. He wrapped her in a hug and buried his face in her shoulder to hide any tears that may have been running down his cheek. When he pulled away, he saw that Anna was also teary-eyed. He could tell that she knew he was leaving. She always knew everything.

"Be safe," was all she said.

"I promise I will."

Mimi took the plate with him as he walked out the door. Ozzie was already waiting in the truck. Mimi didn't look back as he got in the passenger seat. The truck pulled out onto the road and began the four-hour drive to the shore.

Two hours into the ride, neither Mimi nor Ozzie had spoken a word. Even though he was nervous and had no appetite, Mimi forced himself to eat the food his mother packed. He had no idea how long this boat ride would take or when he'd be able to eat again.

Mimi gazed out the window at the dim lights on inside all the small houses. They then drove through Miramar, an area occupied by beautiful mansions. He wondered if this would be the last time he would ever see the Melacon, the broad avenue along the waterfront. After driving by the various government buildings, including the huge Russian Embassy that went on for blocks, they found themselves surrounded by the dilapidated, graffiti-riddled buildings in a poverty-stricken area of the country where prostitutes roamed the streets.

When they reached the seashore, Mimi knew they only had an hour left. He tried to close his eyes and get some rest, but the bumpy road kept him awake all the way to the dock.

Ozzie drove the pickup right by the pier, where a dozen boats were docked for the night, and kept driving toward the much darker beach. As soon as he parked in the shadows, Mimi felt a pain in the pit of his stomach. They both got out of the truck. Mimi reached into the back to grab his bag when he noticed that his hand was shaking. Ozzie walked around so he could hug his son one last time. Neither Mimi nor Ozzie were anxious for the hug to end. A single tear rolled down from Ozzie's right eye.

"Be strong and everything will work out," said Ozzie.

Mimi followed Ozzie down to the shore. It wasn't until they were ten feet away from the water when they saw the twenty-foot-long cigarette boat all ready to leave. Gato approached them. He was a stocky man who spoke with a lisp.

"You bring the final payment, Ozzie?"

Mimi watched his father pull a wad of cash out of his pocket and hand it over. It must have taken Ozzie a month to earn that money. Suddenly, the pain in Mimi's stomach turned into a knot.

"Papa! You can't—"

Before Mimi could object, Ozzie pulled him off the side.

"I've been planning this for a very long time."

"But what about you and Mama?"

"Miguel, this is for all of us. You have the chance to make a future for yourself. We plan to follow some day, but we can't do any of this without you."

Mimi knew this was true. If he remained in Cuba, nothing would change, but in America the possibilities were endless, and all because of baseball. Ozzie pulled Mimi in close and whispered into his ear.

"When you get there, I want you to look up Willie Santos in Miami. Remember that name. Willie Santos. He will help get you settled. Trust him."

They hugged one more time. Ozzie walked back over to Gato while Mimi carried his bag down to the boat. Standing on the shore was one of the twelve other passengers — a Santeria priest who was blessing their boat before the journey. Mimi climbed inside the boat and settled in across from a man and woman who were traveling with their five-year-old son. Mimi nodded. He didn't feel like talking and neither did they. A few minutes later, Gato climbed into the boat and started up the engine.

"It's ninety miles to the Florida Keys. If we can avoid the storm, we should get there before dawn."

As the boat pulled away, Mimi waved to his father on the shore and watched until he disappeared from view. Mimi was left with this horrible feeling that he might not see his family again. He tried to put it out of his mind and turned to look at the ocean ahead. It was pitch black until a lightning bolt lit up the night sky.

CHAPTER 3

The first hour of the journey was smooth, but then it started to rain.

The priest kept his eyes peeled on the horizon and hadn't said a word since they left the shore. The family huddled together in the back of the boat. The terrified boy curled up in his mother's arms while the father, a professor, had been talking nonstop to anyone that would listen as a way to calm his own nerves.

"This new regime nationalized education, public health, and the telephone system, but it's the economy that is destroying the Cuban people. The end of the Soviet Union meant no more subsidies for Cuba. Defection to America is more a reflection of the severe economic crisis than it is a political statement."

Mimi had stopped listening. The waves were getting bigger and everyone struggled to keep their balance. The boat rocked. The water gathering in the bottom of the boat was now ankle-deep. It was difficult to look up because the rain was coming down so hard. He was beginning to panic. *Where are we? How close are we to shore? Will I die out here?* He had no idea.

Gato struggled to keep the boat steady. When another wave crashed over the side, the engine sputtered and died. At that moment, everyone on board could feel hope vanish.

Mimi made eye contact with the boy, who was huddled between his parents in the back of the boat. It was the worst possible place they could be because they were taking the brunt of the rain and the waves. Mimi stood up and offered them his seat. He held the railing tight as he made his way to the back and ushered the family into the more secure position in the middle of the boat.

With the engine dead, they were sitting ducks, helpless and completely at the mercy of the ocean, which was not being kind to the tiny boat. Gato, with some help from the passengers, tried to repair the engine, but their efforts were futile. Mimi was dizzy, nauseous, and on the verge of vomiting, but the waves only got worse. The boat came dangerously close to tipping over before coming to a rest. For a brief moment, the rain let up and the ocean appeared calm. Mimi felt a small glimmer of hope, but then he saw it before anyone else: a giant wave approaching from the side. There was nothing he could do but brace himself and wait as it drew near. The ten-foot-high wave broke and then it hit the boat!

Mimi was slammed into the side of the boat with force. He could feel the pressure crack his ribs. Pain shot through every inch of his body. He reached out and wrapped his arms around the bench. He tried to hang on as the wave almost rolled him right out of the boat. He couldn't breathe for what felt like an eternity, but was probably more like ten seconds in reality. Finally, the water stopped crashing over his head.

Mimi gasped as he took his first full breath of air. He heard the young boy begin to wail a panicked cry for help!

"Mama!"

After what he just endured, Mimi was shocked that everyone else remained inside the boat, let alone the boy who was now precariously perched on the edge reaching out so far that he was about to fall overboard.

Instinctively, Mimi grabbed the boy by the shirt. He felt a pain shoot through his chest. He knew his ribs were broken and maybe something worse, but he managed to hang on to the boy and keep him in the boat. Then he saw what the boy was reaching for. The mother was in the water. As soon as Mimi let go of the boy's shirt, the child went right back to the edge.

What Mimi did next surprised even him. He jumped in the water. As soon as he went under, he feared that he made a mistake, but it was too late to turn back now. His clothes weighed him down so much that it felt like he might not make it to the surface. When he finally broke through, he gasped for air as he tried to get his bearings.

The first thing he saw was the cigarette boat drifting farther away. He then spotted the young mother struggling to keep her head above water. He swam to her and reached out, but she fought him off in a frenzied panic that dragged them both under the water. Mimi had to use all his strength to keep them afloat.

"Tranquilo. Calm down. I'm trying to help."

She finally relented, more from exhaustion than rational thinking, but it allowed Mimi to wrap an arm around her body and turn his attention back to the boat. He tried to swim closer, but the current pulled them farther away.

Mimi could see the people on the boat standing and yelling in his direction, but he was too far away to hear what was being said. The professor heaved a rope that landed ten feet away from Mimi. If he was to let go of the crying mother, he could easily reach the rope and pull himself back aboard, but that would mean leaving her to die. He pulled the young mother along with him as he swam. They inched closer and the rope was two feet within Mimi's grasp. He lunged forward and grabbed the knotted end just seconds before they were bombarded by another monstrous wave.

Mimi was back under the water, jostled within a swirl of white foam. He didn't know if he was upside down or right side up. Before he knew what was happening, he surfaced again. Somehow the rope was still in his hand and the mother had her arms wrapped around his chest. His arm jerked as Gato and the professor were pulling him in. He grabbed onto the rope with two hands. He felt like dead weight being dragged through the mud as they inched their way closer to the boat.

When they finally reached the side of the boat, Mimi used the last of his strength to help hoist the mother back in. With her safely aboard, it was Gato who extended an arm to pull Mimi up and over the side. He collapsed onto the floor of the boat, just now realizing how close he came to dying. He was still struggling to breathe, but he was alive. He stared up at the sky. The rain had stopped and the water was strangely calm. It looked like the storm was over, but the severity of their situation quickly sunk in.

The engine was dead, and they were all alone in the middle of the ocean. Nobody on board spoke a word. They could do nothing but sit and hope that another boat would come along.

Minutes turned to hours. Mimi couldn't keep track of the time. Throughout the night, he kept nodding off to sleep, but he'd wake when someone in the boat moved. Mimi didn't know when he actually fell asleep, or maybe he passed out, but he woke up to feel the morning sun beating down on the back of his neck. It was so bright out that he had to squint. The sound of a fog horn shook his body to the core. He turned around to see a large boat approach. Fast. They were saved, but the moment was bittersweet. As the boat approached, Mimi saw that it read U.S. Coast Guard on the side. Everyone on board knew that the dream was dead. They were going back to Cuba.

By eleven that morning, Mimi and all those on board the boat had been brought back to Cuba and placed in a holding cell. From his spot on the cold concrete floor, Mimi watched the family huddled together. The boy was asleep in his mother's arms. She had her head on the professor's shoulder as he stared out the cell window. Oddly enough, the priest appeared unfazed by the entire ordeal. He sat on a bench in the corner, stoic. For the past half hour, Mimi could hear the police questioning Gato in the next room, but Mimi didn't have the energy to follow the conversation. He was exhausted and hungry, but he also felt something that he had never felt before in his life—beaten. He gambled big and he lost. Now he had no idea what fate had in store for him. For all he knew, he might not be allowed back in the Cuban League. He always knew this was a possibility, but he was not prepared for it.

The guard outside smacked his club against the bars. When Mimi looked up, the guard bent down and slipped a plate of bread and a silver cup of water right by his feet.

"Don't let the others see you eat."

The guard nodded and disappeared down the hall. Mimi recognized the man from somewhere, but he couldn't quite place him. He put it out of his mind and tried to reach for the plate, but every muscle in his body screamed out in pain. He sipped from the cup and took a bite of the bread when he saw the young boy look up. Mimi smiled and slid the plate over to him. The professor nodded a heartfelt thank-you and made sure that Mimi kept a piece for himself.

Mimi devoured the bread quickly. It wasn't much, but it helped. He instantly felt better. As he watched the family pass around the bread and water with enthusiasm, he almost forgot that they were sitting inside a prison cell. Suddenly, he remembered where he previously saw the guard. It was at the stadium yesterday. The guard was the father of the boy he gave the glove to after the game.

Five Years Later

CHAPTER 4

Mimi stood in the back of the small church as the seats began to fill up.

He was now close to thirty years old. His face was fuller and his muscles less defined, but he still carried himself like an athlete. The most noticeable change wasn't anything physical. It was his energy, or lack thereof. Gone was the happy-go-lucky kid who used to throw caution to the wind. In his place stood a grown man who appeared worn down by the burden of regret.

Mimi had been coming to this church with his mother since he was a child, but he had never been to a funeral here before. It made him feel even more out of place. He tried to remain hidden in the back as he watched the line continue to grow behind the casket where his father's body was on display for the congregation. Mimi knew that Ozzie was loved, but he never realized how much until he saw all of these people in tears. One by one, people kneeled in front of the casket to say a prayer.

Ozzie's death hit everyone hard. It was completely unexpected. The previous Monday, Mimi returned home to find his mother in tears. All she could say was that it was an accident. He later learned from Ozzie's coworkers at the plant that it was a train accident. Ozzie was hit on his way home from work. The details were sketchy, which was typical for incidents in Cuba. The night of the accident, Mimi camped out at the police station, but none of the authorities were offering up any information. He suspected corruption, but he knew he was powerless to do anything about it. He couldn't help but wonder whether his attempted defection had something to do with his dad's death. Anna tried to comfort him, but paranoia was everywhere on the island with Fidel in charge.

Mimi watched fifteen of his teammates from the Cuban National Team file into the church and take their seats in the back. After several long appeals, Mimi had joined the team a few months earlier and they were scheduled to make their first trip out of the country tomorrow to play in an international tournament in Mexico. Mimi contemplated skipping the upcoming tournament in Mexico because the authorities had delayed the funeral unexpectedly, but if Mimi wasn't going to travel to Mexico, neither would his teammates. That immediately made the government cooperate and the funeral was scheduled for the day before the team was to board a plane bound for Mexico. Many of these players came from a great distance to be there because they knew Mimi would do the same for them.

Mimi had yet to see his father's body. Earlier that morning, the entire family was able to say goodbye to Ozzie in private before the service, but Mimi remained outside. This was his last opportunity, and Mimi knew that he would regret it if he didn't go up there and kneel before his father's casket, but his legs felt weak. He couldn't move. It wasn't until his brother, Manny, walked up and joined him in the back. No longer did Mimi think of Manny as his chubby younger brother. He was now a well-built nineteen-year-old man who was stronger than anyone Manny knew and also had a bigger heart.

"I think it's time," said Manny.

"I know."

Manny didn't have to say anything else. He left to acknowledge the players who occupied the last pew. Manny was also a member of the Cuban National Team. He was more of an honorary member, but still a member. He didn't have the athleticism or raw talent of anyone else on the team, but he had more heart than all of them put together. He didn't get in the game much, but when he was in there, he made his presence felt and that quickly made him a fan favorite.

As soon as the line to the casket thinned out, Mimi walked up to the front and kneeled in front of his father's casket. Every eye in the church was on him, but he wasn't worried about that. He was just trying to keep it together and stay strong. He could only imagine what his father would say if he saw him break down. After a quick prayer, Mimi stood up and joined Anna in the front pew. It felt like a weight had been lifted. For the first time since learning of the accident, he felt at peace with what happened.

The service was emotional. Mimi stayed strong for his mother. He held her hand and gave her a shoulder to cry on. Mimi never considered himself religious, or put much faith in ceremony, but he appreciated the heartfelt sendoff for his father even though Ozzie practiced a much different type of religion. Ozzie practiced voodoo, something which Mimi thought of as witchcraft. This led to many heated arguments. Ozzie lived his daily life relying on voodoo for important decisions. Over the years, he tried to give Ozzie the benefit of the doubt, but the final straw occurred when Ozzie's voodoo rituals led to animal sacrifice.

After the service, the entire congregation moved across the street to the cemetery where Ozzie was laid to rest. As the priest spoke, Mimi spotted two police cars parked along the side of the road. They had been watching him and his family for a long time. His blood pressure skyrocketed, and all of that anger over his father's mysterious death instantly bubbled back to the surface. He couldn't help but feel that Ozzie's accident had something to do with his own failed defection five years earlier. Everything changed for Mimi and his family on that day when he was captured by the Coast Guard and brought back to Cuba. Mimi and Ozzie knew the risk they were taking, but didn't truly understand the consequences until they were forced to live through it. Being banned for four years from baseball was devastating, but looking back now, that was the easy part. When Mimi returned home after jail, he saw Manny in handcuffs while having a shouting match with a police officer. Mimi and his family became a target for the government. They were harassed and their house was often searched for no reason. They were stopped and frisked when walking down the street. Ozzie was ostracized at work, and Manny was beaten up on his way home from school one day. It took its toll on Mimi and slowly drained any remaining feeling of joy from his life. Knowing that his family was suffering from something he did was more than he could take some days. Without baseball, Mimi began to read more about United States history and culture. American history books were not accessible in Cuba, but through friends at the

University of Havana and the Ministry of Foreign Commerce, he was able to obtain copies of newspapers from the States. He even taught himself to speak some English. Things got worse before they got better, and it was only with the help of his uncle, who happened to be a judge in Fidel's government, that the family avoided a worse fate and helped Mimi get back on the Cuban baseball team.

When the crowd dispersed and moved to Anna's house to eat and pay their respects, Manny stayed behind with Mimi as he said a final goodbye to his father. Mimi thought about how hard his father was on him. Ozzie always saw Mimi's potential as a player, even after the failed defection, and would never let him quit. This led to some intense fights between the two of them, but Mimi appreciated it now more than ever because he knew that Ozzie was partly responsible for the work ethic that helped him reach that potential.

Mimi knew that this might be the one and only time he would visit this grave so he wanted to soak it all in, but no matter how he much he prayed or how many times he tried to say goodbye, it never felt like enough. Finally, he stepped away and that's when he saw Manny approach.

"Mama wanted to make sure I get you back to the house."

"I think I'm gonna walk."

"You sure?"

"Tell her that I'll be home in a half hour."

Manny nodded. He turned and walked back to Ozzie's old truck. Once Manny drove away, Mimi found himself all alone in the cemetery. He took one last look at his father's grave and headed for the exit.

When he left the cemetery, he took a left turn down a dirt road that brought him to the sugar processing plant where Ozzie worked the majority of his life. As he continued down the road, he saw the train tracks off in the distance where Ozzie tragically died. Not wanting to return to the scene of the crime where he spent so much of the past week, he decided to walk in the other direction. He took the long way home and enjoyed his walk through the town and across the baseball field where he grew up playing.

By the time Mimi reached the street where his mother lived, he could already hear the music. There were probably fifty people inside his house. Everyone in the neighborhood was there. So much was happening inside that nobody noticed him when he walked in. It cheered him up seeing his mother with so many people around to keep her company. He watched her laugh with some of the older members of the community while telling stories about Ozzie. He worried about how his mother would be when everybody left and she was all alone in the house. He knew that she would never complain to him no matter how much she was hurting inside, but he also knew that she was the toughest person he ever met so she would find a way to endure.

"I made you a plate."

Mimi turned around to see twelve-year-old Adonis holding up a paper plate loaded with more food than any one man could eat. Adonis weaseled his way into becoming the ball boy for the national team. Nobody ever gave him the position. He just kept showing up to practice day after day to carry equipment, wash uniforms, and do whatever else needed to be done. He did everything, and he was also a good player who was only getting better because he got to play with and learn from the best. He was a sponge.

"Do you think that's enough?" Mimi joked.

"You need your energy."

"Can't argue with that," Mimi said as he took the plate with a smile.

"Quieres una cerveza? Beer? I can get you one."

Everyone was drinking, even a few of the players, but Mimi wanted to keep a clear head. Not only did he have to get up early and travel to the airport, but he knew how vulnerable he was. He feared that drinking today could send him down a dark path so he promised himself that he wouldn't touch any alcohol.

"No hoy," Mimi said as he ruffled Adonis's hair.

Adonis returned to the other players to grab their plates and go fetch them more food. Mimi was happy to see the house full for his mother's sake, but he didn't want to talk to anybody. He took his plate out the back door and set up on the tree stump in the far corner of the yard.

An hour later, he had finished eating, but was still sitting in silence when his teammate, Alejandro Castillo, came out to greet him. Mimi stood to wrap Alejandro in a bear hug. Five years earlier, Alejandro was a hothead third baseman who talked down to Mimi during the last game before his failed defection. Now Alejandro was one of Mimi's closest friends and the man he credited for his comeback.

"How you holding up?" asked Alejandro.

"About as well as you'd think."

"Ready for tomorrow?"

"Not yet, but I will be."

"I don't doubt it, my friend," said Alejandro as he gave Mimi one last pat on the back. "We're all going back to the hotel, but will see you on the plane tomorrow."

As Mimi watched Alejandro and the rest of the players leave the house, he remembered how much he used to dislike Alejandro. He was a great third baseman, but he would lash out at anyone who threatened his rise to be the next big Cuban star. Mimi assumed the feeling was mutual so he was surprised when, after being banned from baseball, Alejandro was the first player to reach out to him. Alejandro actually thanked Mimi for teaching him a lesson that day back in June when Mimi made the all-star third baseman look like a fool for bobbling the ball and allowing Mimi to score. It was good for Mimi to hear that, but the suspension took its toll. When he was allowed to return to the league four years later, he was overweight, out of shape, and lacked the desire to compete. Mimi had accepted the fact that his dream was over and that he'd soon be working at the plant alongside his father. Once again it was Alejandro who reached out. They became close friends, and Alejandro's passion rubbed off on Mimi, who remembered what it was he loved about the game of baseball. Pretty soon Mimi was reinvigorated. It took almost a year for him to get back into playing shape, and he was a step slower, but he was able to play the game with passion and excitement once again. The fans returned and flocked to watch him play. When it came time to select the Cuban National Team, Mimi's name was at the top of the list and Alejandro's was right up there with him.

The police officers remained outside the house until the last of the guests left around 10:00 p.m. Anna fell asleep, so Mimi and Manny stayed up late washing dishes and cleaning the house just like the used to do years earlier. Manny was concerned for his brother because he knew that he blamed himself for so many of the bad things that happened. Manny also knew that there was nothing he could say to make Mimi think otherwise so he had stopped trying.

"I'm going to get some sleep. You should, too," said Manny.

"I will."

They both knew he wouldn't. When Manny's bedroom light went out at midnight, Mimi was still on the couch watching television. He sat there, wide awake, until 5:00 a.m. when he woke up Manny who struggled to drag himself out of bed. They packed their bags and picked at the leftovers in the fridge.

When the van pulled up outside to take them to the airport, Manny carried their bags outside and loaded them into the van while Mimi stayed behind in the house. He walked down the hall and quietly opened his mother's door. Anna was still asleep. He didn't want to wake her. The past twenty-four hours had been such an emotional rollercoaster that one more heartfelt goodbye might be enough to push them both over the edge, so he kissed her on the top of the head and left the room, carefully closing the door behind him. Mimi walked outside and piled into the van, but as soon as they drove away from the house, he regretted his decision.

Two hours later, Mimi and Manny boarded the plane with the rest of the team. As he walked down the narrow aisle, he heard a familiar voice call out.

"I got that!" Adonis jumped up and grabbed Mimi's bag before he had a chance to find his seat.

"You sure?"

"I'm sure."

Mimi laughed for the first time in days as he watched Adonis stand on the seats and struggle to put the bag in the overhead compartment.

Mimi settled into a seat by the window. He took one last look at Cuba before closing the shade and trying to get some sleep. Emotional fatigue had finally set in.

The last person to get on the plane was a pudgy man with deep olive skin and coal black eyes. Once he might have been athletic, but ten extra pounds now hung over his belt, and the muscles in his arms looked soft. Gabriel Fuentes was a member of the Cuban DGI, the island's intelligent service. His job at this time was to shadow the Cuban baseball players who might think of defecting while out of the country. During this trip he would be focused primarily on Mimi, who, even though pushing thirty, had the most to gain by getting to a major league team in the United States.

Fuentes avoided eye contact as he made his way down the aisle to the last row of seats. Adonis didn't jump up to grab his bag. It was difficult to tell if the players were more upset that Fuentes was making the trip, or if Fuentes was more upset for having to come along. This was not his ideal assignment, and he hated Mexico. He took his seat. He pulled a flask from the bag at his feet and began to drink.

CHAPTER 5

Mimi stepped into the batting cage. He dug his spikes into the red dirt by home plate as he looked out at the batting practice pitcher.

This was the first time he had ever set foot in the beautiful Estadio de Beisbol Stadium in Monterrey, Mexico. It was the largest baseball stadium in Mexico, state of the art with video screens, television monitors, and over 300 luxury suites. The 27,000 seat capacity would be in full use on this day. And only 150 miles from the U.S. border.

Mimi's Cuban team was preparing to take on the Mexican National Team in the first round of this international tournament. The buzz currently building in and around the stadium existed in large part because it had only been in recent years that the Cuban government even permitted its powerful national teams to travel abroad to compete.

It was two hours before game time but already a couple thousand fans wandered throughout the stands. Most of them stopped and stared toward home plate as Mimi stepped into the box. His reputation preceded him. The fans came to see Mimi not only because he was considered to be one of the best players ever produced by the island of Cuba, but also because they were aware of what he had gone through trying to defect from Cuba several years earlier and the struggles he endured to get back on the baseball field.

Teammates, including Manny, gathered around the cage for batting practice. The trash talk stopped as Mimi got into the box. He started out on the right side since he would be facing a lefty from the Mexican team. The pitcher let the first ball fly. Mimi swung hard and completely missed. All of the air was sucked out of the stadium. Mimi didn't seem to care. He dug back into the box. When the pitcher threw the next ball, Mimi hit a dribbler that didn't get out of the infield. That was followed by a harmless pop fly, a foul ball into the stands and a weak grounder toward shortstop. Mimi could hear some of the chatter coming from the nearby fans in the crowd who were all wondering what happened to this legendary hitter they heard so much about. Mimi turned around to hit left-handed and things changed as he sprayed solid line drives to left and right field. He took a deep breath, moved back to hit right-handed, and drove the next pitch over the wall in center field. Ever since Mimi's dad taught him to be a switch hitter, he learned that if he was struggling from one side of the plate, sometimes you might be able to find your groove by hitting from the other side. The next few swings Mimi hit weak ground balls and pop-ups, but at least he showed some positive signs. After all, he was still early in his comeback.

Sitting behind home plate, a dozen rows up, was Carlos Zapata, head international scout for the New York Yankees. Zapata, who was tall and hefty with graying hair, turned fifty years old the day before to absolutely zero fanfare. Right now he had a pensive look on his face as he closely watched Mimi take batting practice. He was still convinced that the Cuban center fielder was one of the best prospects he had ever seen and didn't seem to share any of the same concern as the fans who were now grumbling about Mimi being a has-been. Zapata even felt compelled to lean over and interrupt the conversation two executives were having next to him. "Look, I've been a scout for over twenty years. I have seen many of the great hitters, and I put Mimi up there with any of them. He needs to get back into rhythm. You might not be impressed with the results now, but I can still see his bat speed. It's just a matter of timing."

Now even more people in the stands stopped what they were doing to watch Mimi in the cage. He was obviously struggling to make solid contact. Out of the fifty pitches he saw, only about ten would be considered solid hits with one sailing over the fence for a home run.

The fans might have been skeptical, but Mimi appeared unfazed. After his fairly unimpressive batting practice performance, he jogged around the bases, smiling and joking with teammates. Several minutes of stretching then preceded infield-outfield practice, which was an opportunity for him to show off his potent arm from the center field position, but once again, the fans were not that impressed by what they saw. The general consensus was that Mimi was past his prime.

There was still more than an hour until the start of the game so Mimi found solace in a corner of the clubhouse, as he often did before a game. He put his headphones on and began listening to the music of Arturo Sandoval. Sandoval had been revered in Cuba as an exceptional musician until his defection to the United States. He was charged with treason and found guilty according to the Cuban government. They immediately pulled his music from Havana stores. Mimi closed his eyes as he immersed himself into the sounds of this jazz-Caribbean trumpeter who joined the band of the great Dizzy Gillespie on a European tour in 1990 and never returned to Cuba. Mimi smiled as Sandoval's version of Gillespie's "Salt Peanuts" danced inside his head. Mimi leaned back in the locker room's only sofa chair, hands clasped behind his headphones as the next tune, "Be Bop," began. Tears formed in the corner of his eyes as he reflected on life back home and his late father.

"Wake up. *Treinta minutos*."

Mimi opened his eyes and saw Manny standing above him. The locker room was now filled with his teammates.

Mimi slowly returned to reality. He grabbed his glove and followed Manny back out onto the field. As he did before every game, Mimi played catch with his brother, followed by some last-minute stretching. He would be the third batter up to start the game and was excited to be hitting right-handed, his natural side, because lefty Omar Mendez was pitching for the Mexican club. Mendez was the ace of the Mexican pitching staff but did not look much like an athlete. He was medium height, stocky with short arms, and tossed the ball to home plate using a herky-jerky motion, which often baffled hitters.

The crowd roared when the home team took the field. Because they were the visiting team, the Cubans would bat first. It was a beautiful day for baseball. The sun bathed the field in gold under a cloudless sky. The temperature was seventy-five degrees, and there was a slight breeze as the Mexican team took the field and the game began.

When Mimi came to bat in the first inning, the stadium turned dead quiet. Runners were on first and second after the first two hitters singled and walked respectively. Mimi dug in and stared down the pitcher, but stood there with the bat on his shoulder as strike one blew right by him. The pitcher wound up for the next pitch, which snapped into the back of the catcher's glove for strike two. At this point, everyone in the crowd expected strike three to come next and for Mimi to return to the dugout without even taking a swing, but when the pitcher let the ball fly, Mimi whipped his bat around for a picture-perfect swing that sent the ball sailing over the left field fence for a three-run home run. The crowd was stunned. The Mexican team was also stunned because Mimi's mediocre performance in the batting cage wasn't lost on them either. Only Mimi, his teammates, and Zapata were not surprised.

Mimi had set the tone with one swing of the bat. The Cuban team followed up with four runs in the second inning and three more in the third to open up a 10-0 lead that would stand until the end of the game and advance Cuba into the second round. All of the fans had forgotten about what they witnessed during batting practice and were now anxious to see what this Cuban team would do during their next game, but Mimi didn't plan to stick around.

CHAPTER 6

After the game, Mimi nervously walked from the clubhouse to the team bus, which was sitting in the parking lot outside the stadium. He knew he would get special attention. Out of the corner of his eye, Mimi noticed Fuentes leaning against a wall about twenty feet from the bus with a cigar nub in one hand and a pint of whiskey in the other. Mimi did not flinch as he stepped onto the bus joining his teammates as they celebrated the convincing victory over Mexico.

The bus slowly exited the parking lot heading northbound on a dark narrow dirt road. Twenty minutes later, it pulled up to the Hotel El Dorado. Stepping down from the bus, Mimi was greeted by a few autograph seekers and he happily obliged, even engaging in conversation.

When Mimi turned around, Adonis was standing there holding Mimi's bag.

"Estas listo? Ready?" said Adonis with a smile.

"I hope so."

"Okay then, let's go."

"After you."

Adonis turned and proudly walked through the hotel. Mimi followed as they made their way to Mimi's second-floor room. While Mimi fished his key out of his pocket, Fuentes walked down the hall from the opposite direction. Under his arm was a fresh pint of whiskey wrapped in a paper bag. The two stared at each other.

"Big plans tonight?" asked Fuentes.

"A long shower and a lot of sleep," said Mimi.

Fuentes appeared satisfied and disappeared into his room. Mimi unlocked the door and opened it for Adonis, who carried the bag inside. Mimi entered and locked the door behind him.

"He's in. Probably for the night," said Adonis.

"Yes, he is. Sure you're up for this?" asked Mimi.

"When have I ever let you down?"

"I'll owe you, Adonis."

"We'll meet again in America when I'm playing for the Yankees in a couple years."

"I don't doubt it."

Mimi took a deep breath and tried to slow his racing heart.

"Okay, here we go."

Mimi turned on the TV. He turned the volume up loud. He then went into the bathroom and turned on the shower. He grabbed the small gym bag that had been pre-packed in the corner. He kneeled down in front of Adonis and went over the instructions one more time.

"In a half hour turn off the shower—"

"I know. I know. Then walk around the room and make a lot of noise."

"But not too much noise."

"Right. I got you covered in case Fuentes does a room check. Nobody will know you're gone until tomorrow at noon."

With bag in hand, Mimi opened the window and climbed out onto the fire escape. He gave Adonis one last wave before he made his way down the rusty old ladder to the street, careful not to make too much noise.

Once he hit the alley, he casually walked to the main road. Six blocks due west at the intersection of Baja and Minaloa, Mimi saw the burgundy Toyota driven by Jose. Mimi hustled into the back seat of the car. In the passenger seat was a large, bearded gentleman unknown to Mimi. The three of them sped off, heading north toward the United States border near Nuevo Laredo.

"*Que pasa*, Mimi? Everything go okay?" Jose asked.

Mimi let out a sigh and a laugh. "It's not like it used to be. They now got one-half-drunk DGI agent supposedly watching us. Not like that makes decision to pick up and leave any easier, but getting away certainly is."

Mimi looked at the man sitting in the passenger seat and extended a hand. "I'm Mimi."

The man responded in his gravel voice without turning around, "I'm going to call you Dusty . . . as in Dusty Foot." He coughed and chuckled. Jose laughed too, but Mimi had no idea why.

"Don't mind, Felix," Jose said to Mimi. "You are about to be a dusty foot migrant. That's what they call us now when we enter the U.S. from Mexico. That's quite okay though because it's a lot easier than getting there by boat."

"Don't remind me."

"Dusty foot migrants can still obtain legal status under the law. Thank you, President Clinton."

Mimi leaned back in his seat and stared out the window, but he was anxious for the entire three-hour ride to the border. There were several border-crossing stations and Jose knew which one he wanted. They waited in a short line of vehicles. As they reached the front of the line, a tall, skinny young border patrolman approached.

"Good evening, sir," said Jose calmly. "How we doing tonight? Seems pretty quiet."

The border patrolman nodded but said nothing as he pointed his flashlight inside the Toyota. Jose handed him a packet of documents. Mimi, sitting silently in the backseat, tried not to make a sound. The patrolman paged through some of the documents, which were meticulously prepared and proved that the three of them were Cubans seeking asylum in accordance with the Cuban Adjustment Act and United States immigration policy. Jose knew the necessary papers were very much in order.

"Excuse me for one moment," said the patrolman who walked back into the booth where another man was working on a computer. Mimi stared out his window carefully watching as the two patrolmen conferred. His heart started to race. They were so close.

Jose picked up on Mimi's anxiety. "No te preocupes. Everything is fine."

Ten minutes later the patrolman returned. "Please pull your vehicle into the waiting area over here and we will get back to you."

Jose pulled the Toyota slowly into a large designated area, which included a parking lot, bathrooms, and a gray dreary-looking detention center surrounded by armed guards. Mimi wanted to wait until he was safely in America before getting out of the car and going to the bathroom out of fear that something bad would happen, but he couldn't hold it any longer. He stepped out of the vehicle and made his way to the bathroom. He was searched by a guard on his way inside. He recalled the long night five years earlier when they were intercepted by the U.S. Coast Guard and hauled back to Cuba. Once inside the bathroom, Mimi began to panic, but he splashed water on his face to calm himself down and returned to the car. The trio waited for almost an hour before the patrolman strolled toward their car, casually returned the documents. "Have a nice night."

One minute later they were in Texas.

Mimi was at a loss for words to describe the feeling as they drove into the United States of America. He was about to start crying, but laughed instead. He gazed outside the window as they drove along a highway somewhere in Texas. Mimi was in awe as he checked out everything—the buildings, billboards, neighborhoods, cars and people. Felix kept changing the dial on the radio and landed on something known as country music, which sounded strange to their ears. Pretty soon all three of them were laughing.

As Jose stepped on the gas and hit 70 mph going east on Interstate 10, Mimi thought about his mother. She knew he was leaving. Manny knew. A few of the members of Mimi's team knew, but nobody spoke about it. There was the obvious danger associated with the act of defecting a second time, but part of it was also superstition. Having already failed in his first attempt to leave the country, Mimi didn't want to think about what would happen to him and his family if this attempt to leave was thwarted as well. Mimi didn't even want to try defecting a second time, but it was Ozzie who convinced him that this was the best thing Mimi could do for the family. Ozzie laid the groundwork and made the arrangements. When he died, Anna insisted that Mimi follow through with the plan because they all knew what his father would have wanted. This was the best way to honor him.

Mimi, Felix, and Jose had not eaten for hours so they stopped at the first place they came across, which happened to be the Chuck Wagon Diner twenty-five miles outside of San Antonio. It felt good for Mimi to stretch his legs when he stepped out of the back of the Toyota. The three Cuban men walked into the diner. There were about ten customers inside as they took a seat in the back corner booth.

"We play much better baseball than they do in the Dominican," said Felix to Jose as they picked back up their discussion from the car. "It's just a matter of time before the floodgates open and Cuban players will impact major league baseball much like the Dominican."

"Not while Fidel is alive," said Jose. "The guy wields power like a tyrant. No human rights, no dignity, no freedom. Fidel uses the people as his own little ants and worker bees for his benefit. You really think he's going to let the country's best players just leave for America?

"What do you think, Mimi?" said Felix.

"I don't want to think of that right now. We're in America. San Antonio. Let's go see the Alamo. Davey Crockett? Jim Bowie? You guys know about American history?"

Jose and Felix exchanged a look and turned their attention back to the menus.

"Do we go up to the counter and order? What's going on?" asked Mimi.

"I don't think so," said Jose as he pointed to waitress taking an order from people at another table who came in after they sat down.

They looked around and realized that four other customers, who had come in after them, had already gotten their food. Mimi made eye contact with a middle-aged man with long, wavy blonde hair wearing a cowboy hat and sporting a toothpick in his mouth. He was sitting at the counter, giving them a glare that said "who the hell are these three dark guys and what are they doing in our diner?"

It didn't take long for the smile on Mimi's face to disappear. This was not the introduction to America that Mimi had expected. The bigotry was blatant and it hurt.

"Maybe we should just leave," whispered Mimi.

Jose signaled to the waitress for the second time, and Felix grumbled under his breath. Finally, an elderly waitress reluctantly came over and took their food orders. Whatever Jose ordered, Mimi and Felix both said "same thing," having no idea what they were about to eat. As hungry as they were, at this point they just wanted to eat and leave. Mimi had heard and read about prejudice in America, and within a few hours of being in the country, he experienced a small slice of it.

A half hour later, Mimi left the diner with Felix and Jose. They avoided any incident, but their dignity was wounded. It wasn't until they reached the Toyota in the back of the dusty lot that they saw that one of their tires was slashed. They spent the next hour putting on the spare and hoped it would hold all the way to Miami.

The diner closed and the Toyota was the only car left in the lot. As Mimi watched the sun go down, he realized that he would not arrive in Florida on time. His first day in America had not gone as expected.

Florida, U.S.A.

CHAPTER 7

Guillermo "Willie" Santos, agent extraordinaire for Cuban baseball players and the son of Cuban immigrants, stood on the terrace outside his ultra-modern office building in downtown Little Havana, Florida. The terrace is where he comes every morning to check e-mails on his phone. He has been coming to the office for years but never gets tired of the view or watching the foot traffic below him.

Willie stands just under six feet tall, no more than 150 pounds, with a thick dark afro and a nose too big for his face. He has a hyper personality that could only be calmed by lighting a cigar. As a baseball agent, he has a relatively small roster of players, only representing twelve professional players, eight of whom are Cuban defectors. And only a handful of those clients have ever set foot on a major league field, but he has his eyes on some very good prospects. Willie is thinking long term. He knows that talented Cuban baseball players will be flocking to the United States when the impasse between the two countries thaws. When that happens, Willie is going to be ready. He even believes that someday there will be a major league baseball club in Havana and for the eventuality he has actually taken steps. He was putting together a business plan for just such a happening. After all, major league baseball and the NBA had expanded to Canada. In the future it made sense for major league baseball to go south as well. In the meantime, it became a personal cause for Willie to help Cubans come to America, adjust to the lifestyle, and enjoy the benefits.

Willie was born in Miami in 1976. His parents, Maribel Delgado and Andres Santos, were exiles who left Cuba in 1962. They were two of the 14,000 unaccompanied children airlifted out of Cuba by Operation Pedro Pan. That program was intended to provide an opportunity for parents in Cuba to send their children to Miami to avoid the Marxist-Leninist indoctrination instituted by Fidel Castro's takeover. These parents feared that the Cuban government would strip away their parental authority and believed their children would have a better life in America. The United States State Department authorized visa waivers, thereby permitting these children to travel to America. The parents' decision to separate from their children was, of course, the toughest decision imaginable. Maribel never forgot arriving at the Miami airport as a child and then waiting in a lounge until she met the family that would be taking care of her. Then after four long months, her father, Ivan, was able to join her in the United States. They began their American life, doing their best to assimilate into the community of Little Havana.

Willie's parents were strict. They forced him to study and do his chores. Andres worked in an accounting firm and Maribel as a maid. They were determined to provide their little Guillermo with an opportunity for a good life in America. Willie became close with his abuelo, Granpapi Ivan, who was always there when he got home from school or from playing ball. Ivan would do magic tricks with a deck of cards and somehow pull quarters from Willie's ear. They played catch almost every day. They talked about everything, except life in Cuba. Despite Willie's questions, that was a subject that Ivan, like Maribel and Andres, did not want to talk about very much.

Willie graduated from Florida State University with a degree in economics. That made his parents and grandfather so proud. He married a blond-haired, blue-eyed Florida girl named Marilyn, whom he met in college. They had two daughters, Katie and Valerie. Willie took a great deal of pride in being a good family man and father. He made sure he spent quality time with his daughters and even found time to coach his older daughter, Katie, in youth soccer.

Willie's agency was essentially a one-man operation, with the exception of the indispensable Claudia, who worked part-time as his assistant, office manager, secretary, and receptionist. On the office walls were pictures of Cuban baseball players, including Orestes Kindelan, Miguel Valdes, Omar Linares, Livian Hernandez, Orlando Hernandez, Jose Ibar, Rene Arocha, Rolando Arrojo, Rey Ordonez, Minnie Minoso, and German Mesa. Willie could tell stories about each of these players, but German Mesa was his all-time favorite. Many scouts believed Mesa to be the greatest defensive shortstop to ever play the game. He was often compared to Ozzie Smith, and everyone who saw him play had their own personal recollection of a play that Mesa pulled off unlike anything they had ever seen from a shortstop. He combined smooth yet acrobatic feats that defied gravity. In 1996 Mesa was banned from Cuban baseball for supposedly taking money from an American player-agent. He was removed from the 1996 Cuban Olympic team because authorities feared he would defect in Atlanta. He never defected but did mysteriously disappear from the game of baseball.

Willie grabbed his white fedora hat and left the office. When Willie Santos walked down the streets of Little Havana, he was treated like a political candidate running for office. It seemed as though he knew everyone, shaking hands and exchanging pleasantries as he moved along Calle Ocho. Walking past Domino Park, Willie stopped and joked with a few old-timers playing dominos on a table in the park.

"Yo, Chico, how much you gonna lose today?"

Chico pulled himself away from the game to give Willie a handshake and a hug.

"Hoy soy un ganador! Today is my day to be a winner," said Chico as he returned to the game. "We can't all be as smart as you, Senor Universidad."

Willie continued his brisk walk down Calle Ocho. Little Havana had restaurants, fruit stands, cigar shops, art galleries, music spots, and a lot of energy. Social, cultural, and political events were commonplace. Willie always felt the warmth and passion of the residents who showed their unmistakable love for the United States. American flags and other symbols were on display, not just on the Fourth of July, but all year round. Notions of freedom and opportunity were more than just words to Willie and the other residents of Little Havana. As he approached Memorial Park on Thirteenth Avenue Willie stopped to check out the monuments depicting Cuban heroes such as poet and revolutionary Jose Marti. He moved on to the memorial flame honoring the heroes of the Bay of Pigs and then to the Walkway of the Stars paying tribute to artists such as Celia Cruz and Gloria Estefan. Willie had seen all of these symbols hundreds of times over the years, but each day he still felt the same pride and joy that he did the first time he set eyes on them.

Willie entered one of his favorite restaurants, El Pescador, and sat down in his regular booth. Within seconds, a busboy and a pretty young waitress rushed over to their favorite customer. He asked for a coffee but held off on ordering any food. He was often here in the morning, but today was a little different. He was meeting his lawyer, Rafael Velez. They first met each other fifteen years earlier when they had offices in the same building. They were both getting started in their respective careers and had similar backgrounds. Velez was a tall, thin, former athlete who was always impeccably dressed and groomed. He was loud and outspoken, which was the opposite of Willie's more subdued personality, but they clicked immediately. They quickly formed a working relationship when one of Willie's players found himself in a domestic dispute and needed legal representation. Velez even served as Willie's personal attorney from time to time, but lately things had been running smoothly. They were both very busy and hadn't spoken in over a year so Willie gladly agreed to meet his old friend when he reached out.

"I hope you weren't waiting long," said Velez as he slid into the booth.

"Just got here," said Willie as he handed Velez the menu.

"No need. I know it well."

After they placed their orders, Velez explained the reason for their meeting. "Willie, I happened to be speaking to a reporter friend of mine at the *Miami Herald* and heard some disturbing news."

"What did you do now?" joked Willie.

"Not me. You," said Velez with a straight face.

"Me?"

"According to my reporter friend, who almost always gets it right, you are under investigation by the government."

"What could I possibly be under investigation for?" asked Willie.

"Illegally smuggling baseball players from Cuba into the United States."

Willie had a dozen questions run through his mind, but he was so shocked that he couldn't get a single one out. Velez could see that Willie was nervous so he tried to ease his mind, "To my knowledge there has never been criminal charges filed against someone for this. I don't know why the United States Government, with all of its power and resources, is bearing down on a hardworking son of Cuban refugees who escaped the Castro regime. And for what?"

"You can't be serious."

"Apparently the government is about to accuse you of smuggling illegal aliens for profit. The whole thing is ridiculous, in my humble opinion. And it could be BS and never amount to anything."

"Then why are reporters hearing about it?"

"That's what I'm wondering. Let me do some digging and I'll get back to you. I thought you should know, but I don't want you to worry about this."

Willie knew Velez was a great lawyer and he trusted him. They spent the rest of the meal talking about their families. It was good to catch up, but Willie left the restaurant with an uncomfortable feeling in the pit of his stomach.

An hour later, Willie strolled back to the office and found Claudia on the phone behind the small reception desk. She put a hand over the receiver and whispered to Willie, "I have Marc Neufeld of the New York Yankees for you."

"Tell him I'll be right there." Willie had been expecting the call. He disappeared into his office and shut the door. He took a seat behind the desk, put his feet up and grabbed the phone.

"Marco, how ya doing? How are things in the Big Apple today?"

"Calm and tranquil as usual, Willie. How's our boy Mimi?"

"Great. He's on U.S. soil now. We're not sure whether he'll decide to take up residence outside the United States or stay here and subject himself to the draft next month. We have a plan for him to establish residence in the Dominican or Costa Rica so he can be a free agent and we can negotiate with all thirty clubs."

"He is about five years too late. That ship has sailed. He's already thirty years old and when you consider that it's going to take two to three years of adjustment and development, no team is going to commit big dollars to this guy no matter how much talent you think he has. Some people believe his best baseball is behind him."

Willie always thought Marco would be a good poker player. Willie swiveled around in his chair and tried a different strategy.

"I'm not so sure. A few teams have been looking at him. Perhaps the Red Sox will give him a tryout. Maybe they want a World Series more than you do. It has been a while since the Yankees have won one."

Marco chuckled. "Look, the organization has had a special feeling about this guy for some time. Carlos Zapata has followed him for years and loves the guy, but there are others in our organization who think we're crazy to even consider signing Mimi. I'll tell you this though: assuming he's in the draft, we will not use our first or second round pick on him, but we will draft him in the third round if he is available. We would insist on having a pre-draft agreement with you on the amount of the signing bonus. We'll pay high-end third round money. If you decide to take him to the Dominican or Costa Rica to become a free agent, well, you can count the Yankees out, but I'll wish you and Mimi the best of luck."

"I find it hard to believe that the Yankees would have no interest in Mimi just because he becomes a free agent. But anyway, let me know what you mean by 'high-end' third round money."

"That will have to be a future conversation. Go meet with your client. I'll talk to my bosses and we'll circle back around."

"Fair enough."

CHAPTER 8

At six o'clock in the morning, Jose, Felix and Mimi pulled up to an apartment building across from Jose Marti Park on the east side of Little Havana. As he exited the car, Mimi gazed at the beautiful baseball fields, basketball courts, swimming pools, and racquetball courts. Jose could tell Mimi was overwhelmed so he put a comforting arm on his shoulder.

"This is where you'll work out and play ball every day until further notice. Willie provides you with coaches, trainers, equipment, and everything you need. Get a few hours of sleep now and be on the field ready to go at 1:00 p.m."

The three walked up one flight of stairs and up to the door of a two-flat apartment. Jose reached into his pocket for a key and unlocked the door. Inside was a small but nice studio apartment with a kitchenette, basic furniture, and a television. The walls were bare.

Jose and Felix said their goodbyes and a few minutes later Mimi found himself all alone in his new apartment. He took another look around and was so overwhelmed with emotion that he dropped to his knees. Tears formed in his eyes as he thought about all that his father went through to get him here. "If you could only see this, Papi."

Mimi took a shower and did his best to settle in. He tried to lie down for a short nap, but his heart was still racing even though he had only gotten a few hours of sleep. By 12:45, he could hear the noise from the park penetrate the thin walls of his new apartment. Giving up on the idea of a nap, he quickly got dressed and hustled over to the baseball field.

Mimi noticed about a dozen players hitting fungos and playing pepper. He immediately spotted the man in a fedora standing off to the side, watching. When the man saw Mimi approach, he flashed a big smile and gave him an even bigger hug.

"Mimi! I'm Willie Santos. I want to welcome you to Little Havana."

"Thank you. Thank you for everything," Mimi said as he vigorously shook Willie's hand.

"They'll be time to talk later, but for now I want to show you around and have you get loose for about an hour."

Willie introduced Mimi to each of the other ballplayers. They were a mix of college and high school players. He then brought Mimi up to a short, stout coach who had been hitting fungos to a group of players.

"Orlando here will throw you some BP. Probably have you snag some fly balls and run a couple sprints. After, you and I can go back to my office to discuss a few things about your future."

Mimi said goodbye to Willie while Orlando rounded up the players for BP. When it was Mimi's turn to hit, he grabbed a bat and stepped into the box. He may have been in a strange country surround by strange people, but he suddenly felt at home. It reinvigorated him. He had a lot of energy, but as he swung, he could feel the weariness still in his system. He lacked his usual power and his quickness was down. His swing was off. Only by a millisecond, but that was enough. There is only a millimeter difference in hitting the ball squarely, or missing the sweet spot. That's the difference between a pop up and a solid line drive.

After the workout, Willie showed up outside Mimi's apartment in his red Corvette convertible. Mimi climbed in the car and Willie immediately began to speed down the street. After making small talk about the trip and practice, Willie turned serious. "I want you to know that I am here for you in every way. You're going to have some very tough times adjusting, especially off the field. Whatever comes up, whatever you need, just let me know. You can call 24/7. The most important thing to me is that you think of me as a friend you can trust."

Within ten minutes, they reached Willie's building. He parked the car in an underground garage. Once inside the office, Mimi was introduced to Claudia, who gave him a kiss on the cheek and a hug. She left them alone and closed the door on her way back to the reception desk.

Mimi looked over all the pictures on the wall of Willie with various baseball players—some famous and some not. There was also an unusual map of Cuba accompanied by a newspaper clipping describing the game in which the Baltimore Orioles played in Cuba on March 28, 1999. Mimi started to skim the article and instantly remembered that game. Apparently the owner of the Orioles, Peter Angelos, was a big donor to then president Clinton and was able to sidestep the economic embargo. Playing this historic game was a gesture in hopes of improving relations between the countries. Fidel personally greeted each of the Orioles, shaking hands. The Orioles won an exciting game 3 to 2, but eventual defector Jose Contreras pitched eight outstanding innings, striking out ten for the Cuban team.

Willie sat behind his desk, which was filled with pictures of his family, and gestured to Mimi to take the large cushioned chair in front of the desk.

"We have a very big decision to make and it must be made quickly," Willie began. "If you stay here in the United States, you will be subject to baseball's annual amateur June draft next month. That means whichever club drafts you will exclusively own the right to sign you to a professional contract. You are not permitted to speak to or negotiate with any club other than the one that drafts you. However, if you pack up and leave now to take up residency in the Dominican Republic, you will not be subject to the draft and will be a free agent able to negotiate with any or all of the thirty major league franchises. We can arrange that. We have places for you to live and people to look after you. That said, it is not a simple process and there are many rules we must follow to get the necessary approval from Major League Baseball for you to establish residency and to become a free agent. Obviously you'll have a lot more negotiating power as a free agent than as a drafted player, but I cannot sit here and guarantee what will happen out there as a free agent. Players and fans hear about the huge contracts received by certain free agents, but many fall by the wayside. I've had off-the-record conversations with club officials who, primarily because of your age and your time away from the game, doubt that a free agent bonanza awaits you. Also—"

"Sorry to interrupt," said Mimi, "But I don't want to leave now that I'm finally here. I don't care about the money. I just want to get drafted, sign a contract, and start playing ball. Especially if it's the New York Yankees that drafts me, as you seem to think they might. You know that's my dream. You also know how much money I was making playing in Cuba."

"I had a feeling you would say that."

There was a knock on the door. Claudia poked her head inside, "Attorney Paul Hilman is here."

"Send him right in," said Willie.

Hilman entered the office. He was tall and thin with white hair. To Mimi, this guy looked like an attorney. Willie stood up to make introductions.

"Mimi, meet Paul Hilman, who is an experienced immigration attorney and going to help you through the process."

They shook hands, made small talk, and sat back down to sign some papers while Hilman laid out all the information for Mimi.

"I have set up an initial appointment for you at the United States Citizenship and Immigration Services in a couple of weeks. As part of the process, you will be required to undergo examinations by physicians approved by the United States Customs and Immigrations Service, the USCIS. Once that is completed, I will prepare on your behalf an application for asylum and parole."

After a short pause, Attorney Hilman handed Mimi his business card. "Please, discuss this process with Willie. He's very familiar with it. And feel free to call me with any questions. I'll be in touch soon."

Once Hilman left, Mimi felt overwhelmed. "Doesn't waste any time, does he?

Willie laughed. "That's good because I pay him by the hour."

Over the next several days, Willie worked the phones arranging workouts for Mimi. Scouts from six different clubs observed him during his workouts, and some of them requested follow-up interviews. Mimi was nervous and did not feel that he performed at his best either on the field or during the interview process. During interviews, some unusual questions were asked about Cuba, his family, personal life, habits, and possible homesickness. The feedback received by Willie from clubs was mostly positive, but not overwhelming. The Yankees were not one of the teams that arranged a workout or required an interview. Carlos Zapata had seen all he needed to see while scouting Mimi over the last several years. He had also looked into Mimi's personal life and was not concerned.

Two days before the draft, Mark Neufeld called Willie and basically reiterated his club's position that they intended to draft Mimi in the third round, if and only if there was an agreement prior to the draft that Mimi would accept a $600,000 signing bonus. Neufeld also sternly advised, "This is nonnegotiable, Willie. Carlos and I had to fight on our end just to offer you that so do not even consider asking me to go back to them for more. If that figure is acceptable, Mimi would sign a minor league contract and be immediately sent to Tampa where we have a Rookie Ball Club as well as a Class A Club in the Florida State League. No other special covenants in the contract other than a promise to invite him to our major league spring training camp prior to next season. Our plan is for him to complete the current season in Tampa and then go to the Arizona Fall League in October. And I'll need an answer by ten tomorrow morning."

Mimi entered Willie's office at 8:30 a.m. the following morning. Again, Willie knew what Mimi's answer would be. $600,000 was obviously more money than Mimi had seen in his lifetime, but the idea of becoming a member of the New York Yankees organization was even more valuable to the Cuban star.

When Mimi heard the news, he had to fight back tears as he pleaded with Willie, "Please call Mr. Neufeld back and accept the deal."

CHAPTER 9

Willie and Mimi packed to get ready for the three-hour ride to Tampa where Mimi would begin Rookie Ball. Before they left, the two of them stopped at Willie's house to pick up a few items. Sitting in the chair in front of the television was Willie's elderly grandfather, Ivan. Ivan struggled to his feet to embrace Mimi while whispering in his ear. Mimi couldn't really understand what he was saying, but as he looked closely into Ivan's eyes he sensed a lifetime of pain. Ivan kept staring back at Mimi, almost in tears, eventually flashing a toothless smile.

Once Mimi and Willie were on the road, Willie drove his red sports car beyond the speed limit. Willie did most of the talking. Mimi liked Willie. He definitely appreciated everything Willie had done, but he didn't know him very well so he didn't want to get too personal. So when Willie would ask Mimi questions about his family or life back in Cuba, Mimi always tried to steer the conversation away from himself.

"Are all the highways this smooth?" asked Mimi.

"Not all, but most." Willie smiled.

"So many potholes in Cuba."

Halfway to Tampa, Willie stopped at a touristy seafood restaurant on the pier. He parked and they walked up some wooden stairs to a wharf lined with restaurants. As they sat at one of the tables outside, Willie told Mimi, "You'll love this place. Excellent food and a great view!"

Mimi felt sublime looking out at the beautiful blue water as he and Willie ate delicious grilled sea bass and a hearty salad, and drank beer. Willie talked the whole time.

"Even the difficult days serve an important purpose. They make you stronger, better prepared. Just keep moving forward. Work hard. Stay positive. If things don't feel right or good for a day or two, or even three, have faith that it will get better because it will. This is the greatest country on God's green earth. Opportunity, freedom, personal growth, relationships, it's all here for you." Willie took another bite and finished chewing before he continued. "Don't get me wrong, there are some bad people who cannot be trusted, but you must learn to figure that out."

Willie's cell phone rang. He saw who it was and excused himself so he could step away from the table. On the other end of the phone was one of Willie's contacts in Miami who was facilitating Mimi's ability to telephone his brother and mother back in Cuba. Willie was also working with him to obtain temporary visas for Manny and Anna to come to the United States, although there were still many details to be worked out. In the meantime, Willie was able to arrange for an underground courier service to enable Mimi to send money back home to his mother and brother.

In an hour they were back on the road, and by afternoon they passed a road sign that read: "Spring Training Home of the New

York Yankees - Two Miles Ahead." Mimi felt a rush of adrenaline as they approached the stadium. Willie parked the car in the huge lot and the two walked into the facility. They bumped into a trainer who immediately recognized Mimi and gave them a tour of the facility. Mimi didn't say much with his mouth, but he sure did with his eyes as he observed the first-class equipment and the luxurious accommodations the Yankees provided, even at this minor league facility.

When the tour was complete, Willie drove Mimi to the dormitory-style apartment provided by the Yankees, which was less than a mile from the training facility. Entering the complex, Willie stood with Mimi as he registered for his room with the young male employee sitting with a clipboard at the front desk. Once everything was in order, the two stepped outside. "Thanks for the ride. You didn't have to drive me all the way here."

"I should be thanking you for getting me out of the office."

The two hugged and said their goodbyes. When Willie drove away, Mimi walked back into the building and checked out his new room. It was small, but super-modern—like one of the best hotels. He dropped his suitcase and sat down on his bed. While looking out the window at this brand-new country, Mimi felt insecurity and loneliness begin to take hold. Not wanting to let that feeling fester, he grabbed his phone and attempted to call Manny. This time the call connected. His mood changed as soon as he heard Manny's voice on the other end of the phone. It was great to catch up with his brother and learn about everything he had been up to for the past few weeks, but the conversation turned dour when Mimi asked about his mother.

"Ella no se siente bien. She's not doing so well," said Manny. "She misses you. I try to tell her that we'll be able to visit you, but I don't think she believes that."

"We're working on it. My agent says he's trying to get you and Mom a visitor's pass to come here. The Yankees are helping, too. Keep the faith. It will happen, but right now I have no idea how long it will take."

"I know. I know. I believe in you."

Finally, Mimi had to ask about the one thing that had been weighing heavy on his mind ever since he left.

"How bad has it been for you guys?"

"The bars took down all of the posters of you. It said in the newspapers that true Cubans play baseball for the love of the game, not negotiate for dollars."

"I guess that's not a surprise."

"Some Cuban official stopped me in the street the other day. This guy told me that someone was going to knock on your door in America and serve you with a lawsuit."

"My only concern is that they don't hassle you and Mom. And no matter what they say to you about me, don't criticize Fidel or Cuba."

"I know. I know."

"Have you received the money I've been sending?"

"Si. Gracias."

They talked a little bit of baseball before Manny had to leave for work. After the call, Mimi sat on the end of his bed in silence for a very long time. Something about the conversation made him feel even farther away from his family. He knew Willie said he was working to get them out of Cuba, but Mimi feared that he might never see Manny or Anna ever again. He didn't want to think of that possibility so he grabbed his wallet and left the room.

Mimi walked toward the beach. The sun was setting. The orange and gold colors in the sky shone magnificently over the water. He stood still for several moments as he gazed toward his homeland. Day turned to night while he sat alone on the sand and thought of life back home. He remembered how he and Ozzie used to practice until it was dark. They'd walk from the baseball field to the Marx Theatre. Ozzie knew a few of the musicians so they hung out with them between sets. Mimi remembered listening as these artists wondered what their lives would be like if they were allowed to play the music they wanted, where they wanted, instead of having to play music to accompany the Russian and Polish circus. They spoke about their hero, defector Arturo Sandoval, who played incredible, creative music in Miami, even winning Grammy awards. Defecting to the United States was always romanticized, and now, here Mimi was, sitting on the shore of a beach in the United States where he was free to do and say whatever he wanted, but he felt empty inside. He started to wonder if he made the wrong decision.

CHAPTER 10

Mimi played Rookie Ball for ten days before he was promoted to the Tampa Yankees in the Florida State League.

In Rookie Ball, Mimi played with and against much younger players. Most of them were eighteen to twenty years old, and while many had talent, Mimi's age, experience, and baseball maturity gave him an edge. He dominated. The Florida State League was definitely a step up in class, but it was still comprised primarily of twenty-one- and twenty-two-year-old prospects who were not as polished in their baseball skills as Mimi. Moreover, Mimi came to realize that these guys had not lived and breathed baseball for twelve months a year like he did growing up in Cuba. These guys actually played other sports and had other interests. Mimi, on the other hand, never played other sports, or had other interests. He learned that there exists an observable difference in the way baseball oozes from the pores of someone who plays the game 365 days a year compared to another who plays the game seasonally.

Mimi made a splash during his first couple weeks in the Florida State League. He was batting over .400 and had put together a string of All-Star caliber plays in the outfield that left the fans in awe. He was playing well, and he relished the time he spent out on the field because it was the only time when he felt normal and in his element.

Willie had warned Mimi that his transition off the field might be difficult, and even though Mimi certainly didn't expect it to be easy, he didn't anticipate what he encountered in Tampa. He quickly learned that "off the field" included the dugout.

There were only two other Latino players on the team and one Latino coach, which was strange because Mimi was led to believe that more than 30 percent of the professional baseball players in the States were Hispanic. This created a barrier. On the field, everyone spoke the universal language of baseball, but Mimi's different background and broken English made it difficult in the clubhouse.

Mimi found a kindred spirit in right-handed reliever Shin Hasaki, who was from Japan. He didn't speak a word of English. Neither of them felt like they belonged with the rest of the team, and they couldn't communicate with each other, but there was an unspoken understanding between them because each one knew what the other one was going through, more so than anyone else in the clubhouse.

Mimi desperately wanted to speak to Shin about his funky sidearm pitching delivery. He made an attempt when the two found themselves sitting next to each other on a bus ride home from Dunedin after Tampa won a ten-inning nail biter to end an extended road trip. While everyone else on the bus was asleep, Mimi got Shin's attention. He made some sidearm gestures and then pointed at himself while displaying his batting stance. Mimi wanted to know how Shin would pitch to him. Shin understood. He had Mimi stand up in his stance and gestured with his right palm low and away to mean "changeup," then up and in to mean "fastball" since Mimi was a left-hand hitter with power. It was short, but they were able to communicate and that was a joy for Mimi.

Mimi may have felt all alone, but he gave the Tampa Yankees a shot of life and helped them win six in a row while out on the road. They were now on their way home, and nobody was happier than Mimi. Even though his play didn't show it, he was worn down by the travel schedule. It would still be a few days before he could get any real rest. The bus pulled into Tampa at 2:00 a.m., and the team had to be on the field at 10:00 a.m. the next morning.

The team's ace starting pitcher, Billy Cunningham, was scheduled to start, which usually meant it would only take a few runs to get the win. Billy was six feet four inches tall and 225 pounds. He was a good ol' boy from Texas and threw in the high '90s with a nasty slider. Back in college, he dominated hitters more than anyone since Roger Clemens. One year earlier he was the Yankees' first round pick and, after receiving a signing bonus of $3.75 million, was on the fast track to the major leagues. Billy was a cocky, funny, talented kid, and one of the few Americans who tried to reach out to Mimi.

Billy was already out on the field doing his stretching when Mimi went to snag some fly balls in the outfield before the game. Billy yelled out to Mimi, "Don't be afraid to make some great catches today for me. And if you want to throw somebody out at second, third, or home, that's okay, too."

Mimi smiled appreciatively. Later during warm-ups, Billy looked over at Pete Tolley, the left fielder for the Fort Myers Miracle, as he screamed toward Mimi, "Hey, Fidel, how was the boat ride over?"

Mimi was used to hearing stuff like that from fans, but had not yet encountered any of these insults from players. Still, this was tame compared to what he experienced in Cuba, so he ignored it and it was completely forgotten by the start of the game.

In the bottom half of the first inning, Billy struck out the first two batters. When Tolley entered the batters' box, Billy smiled and looked briefly out at Mimi in center field. He then wound up and threw a very hard, very high, and very inside fastball. Tolley tried to duck, but it smacked him square in the back. He groaned and stumbled, almost falling. Tolley looked out at Billy on the pitcher's mound who stared right back at him. Tolley had no doubt that Billy threw that fastball at him on purpose, but nothing had happened yet in the game that would lead the umpire to conclusively determine that it was intentional.

"Take your base," said the ump.

Mimi knew that Billy was looking out for him and that gave him a feeling he hadn't experienced since he arrived in the United States. It was one of camaraderie with his teammates. It made him want to play the best game of his life for Billy, and he didn't disappoint. His three-run homer in the sixth inning gave his team a lead that they never relinquished. Once Mimi crossed home plate, Billy was the first one out of the dugout to congratulate him.

In the days that followed, Mimi and Billy developed a friendship even though they barely spoke to each other. In the clubhouse, they joked around together, and this had a positive effect on team morale. Billy even tried out his Spanish, but that wasn't very successful.

During his day off, Mimi went down to Willie's office to go over his investments, but they ended up having a lengthy talk about baseball. Mimi suddenly felt very comfortable lying on the couch in Willie's office and being able to talk about the sport he loved in his native language. After about an hour, Mimi confided in Willie about his own troubles off the field, particularly communicating with the other players and even the coaching staff. Willie clearly sympathized, and had been expecting this. "Teams have been slow to hire enough bilingual coaches, but it's getting better. A few clubs have set up an entire division devoted to helping Latino players by teaching English, explaining cultural differences, and handling the media."

"Not the Yankees," added Mimi.

"If you think that's bad, a few years ago the Twins had this up-and-coming Latino player. He was their number one prospect so they had invested millions of dollars to sign him, but they did not have one bilingual coach and didn't take any steps to help his development. I've raised this issue to general managers before, but they don't fully understand the unique challenge Latino players face when they come to the United States."

"There are only two other Latin players on our club," Mimi said. "Hector is from Puerto Rico and Benny from Venezuela, but they don't want anything to do with me. In some ways they're even harder on me than the Americans."

"They may be jealous that you received a decent signing bonus," said Willie.

Mimi hadn't even thought about that. Money never factored into the Cuban game because there wasn't any of it, so it never came between teammates like it could in America. This was another part of the American game that was completely foreign to Mimi.

Willie explained, "Here, players are treated differently depending on what round they were drafted and on how much of a signing bonus they received."

"I hear guys tease Billy Cunningham all the time for receiving a multimillion-dollar signing bonus, but he just laughs it off. This one guy the other day told Billy it was time to change his diaper, and everyone began laughing hysterically. Even the coaching staff and the trainers treat him differently."

"Early round picks are definitely put in better positions to be successful than late round picks or undrafted players because the organization has more of an investment in those players."

"To me, everyone should be treated the same and judged by their production on the field."

"That's true," agreed Willie. "But remember that not all of these players pan out. You might be surprised by the number of early round picks that never make it to the major leagues and the number of late round picks that do."

Before Mimi realized it, another hour had gone by. Claudia had left the office on her break, and Willie was already late for his lunch so he had to lock up for the day. On their way out, Mimi asked Willie, "Mind if I give you a call in a day or two?"

"You can give me a call any time you want," said Willie with a smile. Mimi could tell that he meant it, too.

When he got outside, Mimi realized that he had nothing to do and nowhere that he needed to be that day. This was his first full day off in weeks so before driving home, he decided to walk around downtown Tampa. He was feeling more comfortable in America. This wasn't home, but he was starting to find his way. He just needed some guidance, and he realized that he might have just found that in Willie. He trusted Willie even though he found it hard to trust anyone he met in the United States.

Mimi walked passed a mini-mall and decided to go inside. He bought something to eat in the food court. He sat down with his tray and enjoyed watching the people as much as he did eating this strange Chinese food. When he saw young children with their mothers, his thoughts drifted back to his own mother. His last conversation with Manny left him unsettled. He worried about Anna. It bothered him that he couldn't be there with her, but he wanted to let her know that he was thinking of her so he decided to take advantage of being in the mall to buy something he could send home.

Mimi ventured into a department store. He marveled at its size as he walked down the aisles. He quickly got lost, but didn't really care because there was so much to look at and see. He wandered over to the glass case with about two dozen watches inside when a young clerk approached.

"Can I show you anything?"

"Something for my mother," said Mimi

Mimi was nervous that he wouldn't be able to communicate with the clerk, but the young man signaled Mimi to wait a moment. He walked away and returned with a young associate who spoke a little bit of Spanish. Mimi told her all about his mother, and they spent the next ten minutes picking out a watch that he could buy her. Mimi didn't mind spending $500. He had more money now than he had ever dreamed of, but he hadn't been able to spend any of it yet. What better way to enjoy this new wealth than being able to buy something for his mother?

With the transaction complete, he thanked the clerk and continued to walk all around the store. After several minutes he headed for the big glass doors that led to the parking lot, but on his way outside, the alarm sounded and a red light flashed. He was startled and froze in place. His first thought was fire. Then he saw two big white security guards in matching uniforms heading right for him. The first guard did all the talking while the second stood back and observed.

"Can you step over to the side please, sir."

"Me?" Mimi was confused.

"Yes. And may I see the bag?"

The first guard didn't wait for Mimi to respond. He snatched the bag out of his hand and looked through it. His eyes narrowed with suspicion when he saw the receipt. He walked over to his partner and whispered in his ear. The second guard picked up his walkie-talkie, and before Mimi knew what was going on, he was being escorted back through the store and through the doors marked "employees only" to the tiny security room.

The next hour was a blur as the two guards sat down across from him.

"Where did you get the cash to pay for this?"

"Do you sell drugs?"

"Do you know people who do sell drugs?"

"Are you employed?"

At first Mimi was reluctant to tell them that he was a professional baseball player. Once he was in that room, he thought back to his days five years earlier when he was frequently interrogated by Cuban officials. The rule was always to cooperate but not to offer up more information than necessary because it could be used against him. In this case, it eventually became clear that they thought Mimi was something he wasn't, so the truth would actually help him. He slowly explained to them that he was a baseball player for the Tampa Yankees. The two security guards left the room to verify the information. They returned five minutes later with the bag containing the watch he purchased and told him he was free to go.

Mimi walked back through the store, and locked eyes with the nice female clerk who spent so much time helping him pick out the watch. She quickly diverted her eyes and looked away as if he were a criminal or did something wrong. Mimi felt humiliated. He rushed for the exit as quickly as possible. It was already dark out when he reached the parking lot.

It took him ten minutes to walk back to his car. When he finally got home that night after the long drive, he didn't turn the lights on when he got inside. He put his bag down on the table and lay down on the bed. He stared at the ceiling for hours, and was still up at 2:00 a.m. His original plan was to be asleep early so he could wake up refreshed for practice, but the day had taken an unexpected turn.

CHAPTER 11

By mid-August, Mimi had played in thirty games in the Florida State League and had 12 home runs, 26 RBIs, and a .312 batting average. He also had eight stolen bases and was doing his thing in center field. There were rumblings that he might get a September call-up to the major leagues, even though that was not the original Yankee plan.

Even the fans started to take notice. Before one home game, Mimi was in the outfield stretching when he heard several people scream at him from the right field stands.

"Mimi, we love you!" He looked their way and noticed a very pretty brunette yell at the top of her lungs. "Come and talk to us."

Mimi walked over to the group. They became very excited as he signed autographs.

"You're our favorite player," said the brunette. "We're starting a fan club and calling it the Screaming Mimis. We got shirts and everything." Several members of the group were wearing white T-shirts that read "Screaming Mimis" on the front and "Mijares" on the back, along with his number. That brought a big smile to his face.

"Thank you very much for your support. I'll try to make you proud today."

"Meet up with us after a game some time," the brunette said. "We'd love to hang out with you."

"Yeah, maybe."

That day, Mimi went out and played another great game with three more hits and a game-saving catch in center field. This one was a pitchers' duel won by the Tampa Yankees 2 to 1. When he made the catch to end the eighth inning, Billy Cunningham gave Mimi a huge bear hug as he ran in from the outfield toward the dugout. "You are the man!" bellowed Billy.

Mimi was now in the habit of calling Willie right when he walked in the door to talk about the game, but this day he had something very specific on his mind.

"Our hitting coach, Yolanda Miranda, is trying to take the credit for my success," said Mimi.

"Typical stuff." Willie laughed.

"He's our only bilingual coach, but his Spanish is only so-so since he was born in the United States. He tells the press how he's working with me on certain hitting techniques. None of it is true. I hardly ever talk to the guy."

"Many of these minor league coaches are just trying to move up the ladder. They're thinking about their own careers. He's trying to look good at his job, not necessarily to be good at his job. Forget about him and focus on why you're there. You have the Arizona Fall League after this, and if all goes as planned, you'll head to major league spring training camp next year."

"I know."

"But you have to perform. It makes no difference what Yolanda tells the press."

Mimi became pensive for a moment. "I love the game so much. I'm consumed by it, but the more I think about it, the more I realize that there is a lot I have to learn."

"And now you're learning what it's like to approach baseball as a professional. It's a day-to-day grind. The best thing you can do is play the game hard and play the game the right way. Don't just rely only on your talent."

"I've always been a professional."

"But not here. You're dealing with the scrutiny of daily written scouting reports and thousands of fans evaluating every move you make. That's not something doctors, lawyers, cops or someone who works a normal everyday job has to go through. That's not even considering the fact that you just moved here from another country. Not only are players like you going through the language and cultural adjustments, but the added burden of leaving your homeland and family possibly forever. Cut yourself some slack and remember how difficult what you're doing is."

"These Americans play the game a little nastier than I'm used to," said Mimi as he shifted gears. "They have a different mentality."

Willie laughed.

"No, I actually like that. Base runners go after middle infielders to break up a double play. Pitchers intentionally hit batters. Collisions at home plate get violent. It definitely makes the game a little more intense."

"It's just another way players will try to get in your head. The best players in this game stick to their daily work routine. They learn not to let outside forces get to them. They don't let the players, media, umpires, or even the coaches get in the way of their progress."

"How about the fans? Did you see them out there today?"

"I did," said Willie. He paused as he chose his next words carefully. "Enjoy it. Laugh about it. But I advise you, Mimi, ignore the groupies that are out there looking for ballplayers."

"I know. Don't worry. I'm not thinking about them. Right now, I'm only concerned about baseball."

CHAPTER 12

One midsummer day, Mimi left the baseball field after a tough loss in which he went hitless. He did not want to return to his room, so he decided to go for a walk on the beach. It was dark now, and he found himself all alone. As the waves crashed to the shore, he looked out across the dark waters toward Cuba. It felt like the memories of his family and his homeland rolled in with the tide.

Things did not get any better as the days went on. Mimi went into a 0-for-14 slump, including seven strikeouts. His defense and base running also seemed to lack its usual focus and aggressiveness.

Mimi was in a rut. After games and practice, he would come back to his room and stay inside all night. When he eventually did fall asleep, he had some bizarre nightmares that blended life in Cuba with life in America. One recurring nightmare had him ack in his Havana apartment as a very young boy. His brother nny was an adult and his mother Anna was in a wheelchair le to communicate. She was wearing a Yankees hat and n the dream, he was outside and he'd see her stare ou window. Once she set her eyes on him, she would wheelchair faster and faster toward him. That's when Mimi would wake up in a cold sweat.

More often than not, Mimi couldn't sleep at all. Insomnia scared him because he had never experienced anything like it. He just laid there for hours on end with his mind spinning, random thoughts roaming through his head as he stared at the ceiling. It didn't matter how tired he was after a game, he couldn't sleep because his stomach would churn and his mind would wander.

Even when he played well, doubt crept back in. He was swinging the bat decently but still felt his timing was off. He knew that he wasn't getting around on a good inside fastball and was misjudging the curveball just off the plate. A hitter never wanted to be "in-between," so Mimi started to make adjustments. He got in his own head. At first he tried to forget about the curve and just look for a fastball every pitch. He told himself that he would go back and try to adjust to the curve once his timing and confidence returned, but it never did. Things got worse.

When he was unable to sleep, Mimi started watching a great deal of late-night talk shows. American politics fascinated him, so he devoured political talk radio and television. He listened to right-wingers Sean Hannity, Rush Limbaugh, and Bill O'Reilly, as well as left-wingers Rachel Maddow and Thom Hartman. Barrack Obama was in his first year of being president, which was n amazing and historical event, but already Obama was being icized by both the right and left. Mimi had not developed any g political views, and he didn't understand the level of the n toward the president, but it was wonderful to see that had freedom of speech and that there existed freedo of the press. The facts and the truth didn't always seem to matter, but at least watching and listening to these political television and radio talk shows temporarily took his mind off his insomnia.

When Willie called on Wednesday night, the level of depression had increased. Mimi was not in the mood to talk about his loneliness, so he guided the conversation toward American politics.

"Four months after the first black president is sworn in, everyone seems mad at him. The right-wingers say he is a socialist and a communist. They even compare him to Hitler while the lefties say he is a corporate sellout who hasn't lived up to his promises. I love that everyone can say what they want because it's so much different from where I come from."

"You're right, it's crazy and difficult to predict where this Obama presidency will go," said Willie. "There are still a lot of racists out there who don't even accept that he is our president."

"A lot of people think Obama wasn't even born here and therefore is not a legitimate president," continued Mimi. "One of your cable news channels keeps reporting that, even though all of the evidence is to the contrary. What is that about?

"Even his supporters are mad, blaming him for hiring many of the same people who caused the financial collapse when Bush was president."

"I don't know whether I agree with Obama on his policy issues, but I have to give him credit for the way the criticism just seems to roll off him. He is so measured, trying to find consensus, but the Republicans just want to bring him down. I guess freedom allows the people to say stupid, even outlandish, untrue things."

"A lot of people use that freedom for worthwhile purposes, and a lot of people abuse it," added Willie.

"I find it all fascinating because this could never happen in Cuba where the government controls the media. The internet is not even big over there right now."

"The internet is too dangerous for the Cuban government," said Willie.

"I think the internet is great, but it allows a lot of whackos to bring their opinions into the public sphere. In Cuba, the people receive education and healthcare, but in exchange the government owns you and your freedom. I mean, what is the purpose of having free education if you are not free to read what you want and express what you want?

"Here in the United States freedom of speech is paramount, even if it means anybody can say anything whether it's true or not. At least this inspires important discussions and debates. That's a good thing, right?"

"I'm sure it is, but I don't get it, so I better stick to thinking about baseball right now."

That night he slept a little better, but it didn't help him on the field the next day. The team won, but Mimi went 0 for 4. While out in the field, he couldn't help but notice that his fan club had dwindled. The Screaming Mimis were not as enthusiastic as they once were, and that, for some strange reason, made this rough patch seem all the more real. Mimi wasn't speaking to his teammates or coaches very much. Loneliness caused his mind to wander and he knew the mental side of baseball was the most challenging so he needed to figure out a way to stop his wheels from spinning

There was one bright moment during the game. It happened when Mimi was in the outfield warming up before the start of the eighth inning. When the umpires signaled they were ready to begin, Mimi always tossed the ball he was warming up with to a fan in the stands. When he turned toward the bleachers, he spotted a beautiful Latina girl in a Yankees jersey sitting in the first row. The girl was a knockout. She had the most beautiful smile, and she was smiling at him. Mimi smiled back as he tossed her the ball. She even made an athletic catch that impressed Mimi. *Who was this girl*?

Mimi was definitely distracted. He could not take his eyes off her for the rest of the game. Luckily he only had one more inning in the field because he had trouble concentrating on the game. He kept looking over at the girl, and he found himself laughing when they locked eyes. He definitely needed to be cheered up because there had been very little else during the recent games that was worth remembering.

Two days later, Mimi joined Willie at a park downtown. It was a lovely park with palm trees. As they sat at one of the many chess tables, Mimi finally opened up about his slump. "Sometimes, the game seems so easy. It's like the pitch is coming at you in slow motion and the baseball seems like the size of a grapefruit. Other times, it seems more like the size of a pea and is by you before you have a chance to react."

"There is no way to avoid the tough times. You're going to struggle and you're going to fail. The best hitters in the history of the game fail seven out of every ten at bats. What determines your worth is how you deal with those struggles. So much of this game is mental. It's about confidence and your outlook."

Willie could see that his pep talk wasn't helping. "Maybe you've just hit temporary wall. We've talked about this before. We knew there would be struggles."

"I'm struggling emotionally. Crazy thoughts are going through my head." Mimi looked sad. "I often wonder if I did the right thing by leaving my mother and family. I know they will have to suffer because I escaped."

"There is no denying that there are significant adjustment challenges for every player coming here from another country. You have to confront issues of language, culture, food, and prejudice on a daily basis. And for a Cuban defector, these challenges are exponentially more difficult than those from Venezuela, Dominican Republic, Puerto Rico, Mexico, or Panama, Japan, or South Korea. Back home, those guys are viewed as heroes, and their family members can join them in the United States. It's different for the players from Cuba."

"I know. I'm a traitor who deserted my country and shamelessly betrayed the trust placed in me by the Cuban people," Mimi said, almost in tears. "My brother probably isn't even telling me half of what they're going through."

"None of it is easy. I'm sure every man who defects sometimes has the same thoughts you have right now, but in the long run you will be so much more fulfilled. Fidel continues to make everyone's life miserable in Cuba. He's brutal."

Willie could tell that nothing he said was getting through to Mimi, so he changed tactics. "I never told this to anyone, but my mom saw her own father dragged from his home, screaming and crying. She looked out the window of their apartment only to see two members of Fidel's army beat him to death with clubs. They thought he was working for the Batista regime. During the revolution, Fidel's strategy was to saturate the airwaves and schools with support of his regime propaganda. Fidel would not tolerate anyone claiming a business for himself. No more private property. My dad used to tell me about this elderly black man he would see every day on the same street corner running a shoeshine business. When Fidel came, even that old man vanished. No more capitalists. Share equally. Anyone who failed to work got nothing, not even to eat. There's no such thing as working for yourself or your family. Everyone works for everyone else and everyone owns everything together."

Mimi knew Willie was right. He told himself that he was going to pull himself out of his funk one way or another.

CHAPTER 13

On Tuesday at 10:00 a.m., Willie walked into the office of Pastor Juan Carlos Garcia at St. John Bosco Catholic Church for a prescheduled meeting.

Willie, Marilyn, and the kids were Sunday regulars at the church, which was located just outside Little Havana. Two days earlier, Willie had intently listened to a passionate sermon given by the pastor focusing on a Florida law that made it a crime for anyone to knowingly aid or provide housing for an illegal immigrant. It was obviously something that consumed the pastor because he continued on the topic at the start of their meeting.

"Such a law puts the Church in an impossible position," exclaimed Pastor Garcia. "If a person comes to our door in need of assistance, what does Jesus tell us to do? Ignore that individual? I don't think so. Worse yet, are we supposed to report that person to the authorities? As you know, we often provide shelter for the homeless, and food for the hungry. We do not conduct an investigation into the background of every individual who enters our Church seeking help. That is not our calling."

Willie complimented the pastor on the sermon, but that was not the reason for his visit. He got right to the point.

"I know you're a respected man in the community and, for that matter, in the country. I also know that you have a good friendship with Cardinal Mercado. The cardinal has spent time in Cuba with Castro and others in that government. I was hoping you and the cardinal could help influence the Cuban authorities to permit a visit to the United States for two family members of a client of mine."

The pastor smiled. "You're talking about Mimi, aren't you?"

"His mother and brother are dying to see him. It would mean so much to the family if they could be reunited, even for a short time. Miguel's state of mind right now is fragile, and I believe such a reunion would lift his spirits and have a very positive effect on everyone."

"I'm not sure if I can help, but I can tell you this: there is some progress in this area going on under the radar. I really don't know how it might work in this case, but let me see what I can do. I am supposed to see the cardinal at a conference next week in New York."

"Thank you so much!" said Willie.

As the cardinal escorted Willie to the door, Willie got an idea. "How would you and the cardinal like to go to Yankee Stadium for a game while you're in New York? It can be easily arranged."

Pastor Garcia smiled. "We have several meetings scheduled, but I do know that the cardinal is a very big baseball fan."

That both surprised and pleased Willie. The two men embraced, and Willie left the church office. When Willie returned to his own office, he immediately called Mark Neufeld.

"Mark, I have an idea that will help both of us. I'll need you to leave a couple of tickets for religious leaders. Maybe throw in some royal treatment. I know you could use a few points with the Man upstairs."

"What is it you're up to?" asked Neufeld.

"Don't worry about it. Just do this and I'll owe you."

Willie spent the next couple days working diligently on applications for Anna and Manny to obtain exit visas so that Mimi could be reunited with his family. Until recently, the Cuban government had unequivocally rejected their applications, but Willie had heard from one of his sources about a possible breakthrough. The process to get such visas was long and complicated. It also required the permission of both the United States and Cuban authorities. What Willie learned was that it helps to spread a little cash around. Money, in both capitalist and communist countries, is the lubricant that often gets things done. Communist officials, despite their ideology and protestations about caring for the poor, care as much about money as the most voracious Wall Street investor. In fact, Willie read an article in *Forbes Magazine* that estimated Fidel Castro was worth about $20 billion. The fondness for cash extends to lower-level communist officials, who are always open to bribes.

After a long day of work on a Friday night, Willie was ready to leave for the weekend when he received a call from lawyer Rafael Velez, who suggested they meet the following day. *On Saturday?*

This can't be good, thought Willie. "I have my daughter's softball game tomorrow afternoon. Can we push until Monday?"

"Let's meet for breakfast," said Velez. "I'll be with my associate. We have a lot to go over, but assure Marilyn I'll get you to the game on time."

Willie didn't argue, but he was concerned that this case was becoming more serious than he originally thought. He didn't want to worry Marilyn, but she could tell something was wrong and did a good job of not letting his mind race that night.

The next day, Willie arrived early at El Pescador to see that Velez was already sitting at a table next to a petite brunette with horn-rim glasses.

"There he is!" said Velez as he stood up to shake Willie's hand. "I want you meet one of our firm's rising stars, Ms. Joanna Zall."

"It's a pleasure," said Willie as he pulled up a seat.

After the waitress took their orders, Velez talked about Joanna's recent rise in the firm. She was just two years out of Georgetown Law School, where she graduated with honors and was the winner of the legal writing award. Her father was a senior partner in the law firm of Schaffer, Hardy, and Katz, which had offices in Boca, Washington, D.C., Chicago, and New York. She could have worked there or for one of several other large law firms that offered her employment, but chose to work for Mr. Velez because she thought it would be a more hands-on experience, particularly in cases involving civil liberties.

Willie almost forgot why he was there, but once their food arrived, Velez broke the bad news. "This threat might turn out to be real."

"How so?" asked Willie.

"I think there is a good chance that the government will pursue these charges."

"Okay, so what does that mean?"

"Right now it means nothing. We're going to prepare. I wanted you to meet Joanna because she's coming off a case that could be relevant to your situation and has spent quite a bit of time learning everything there is to know on the subject."

"That case was different than yours," said Joanna, "but we went into a significant amount of history regarding the United States-Cuba relationship because it helped explain why our country favors compassion toward Cubans who defect here as evidenced by our immigration policies."

"She immersed herself in the Cuban Adjustment Act," added Velez.

"Sounds like a blast," joked Willie.

"I was actually really excited to learn," said Jo. "My parents were so obsessed with the Kennedys. There were dozens of books in our house about John, Jackie, and the whole Kennedy clan. My dad admired JFK, and my mom was in love with Jackie. I used to listen to them talk about the assassination for hours."

"I feel like I'm in good hands," said Willie.

"Nothing but the best for you, my friend," said Velez. "But if charges are filed, we're going to establish our position that you did not arrange for Mimi to defect and that you reasonably believed that as soon as Mimi and the others touched land in the United States, their presence was lawful. The facts and the law will prove that regardless of whether or not Mimi had prior authorization to enter the United States, once he did arrive on our soil, he was lawfully entitled to seek political asylum and remain in the United States to play professional baseball. That is to say, you were unaware that the ballplayers did not have permission to come to the United States. In support of this position, we will argue that the Cuban Adjustment Act and the wet foot, dry foot policies of the U.S. Citizenship and Immigration Services make it reasonable for you to have believed that the players could be brought here legally. These factors negate the necessary willful conduct the prosecution needs to prove in order to convict you."

Willie tried to digest it all, but he felt overwhelmed. "Okay, what do I need to do now?"

"Nothing," said Jo.

"But we'll be ready if the government decides to move forward," said Velez.

"I know there hasn't been a case like this before," said Willie with concern. "But what is the worst-case scenario if this goes wrong?"

Velez exchanged a look with Jo and said, "Get that out of your head. That won't happen."

Willie knew that he was in good hands, but he was concerned.

CHAPTER 14

Anna was only fifty-four years old, but was beginning to act, look and move around more like she was seventy. Tall, athletic, light skinned, and pretty, Anna used to run track, but now she rarely had the energy to put on makeup or even brush her hair. The oppressive regime sucked the life out of her. If you were a friend of Fidel, you could do well financially, but if you were an average man or woman, one of the masses, the revolution did not serve you. She always assumed that revolutions were supposed to be fought in the name of the people, the citizens but….

Then she lost a son.

He left without so much as a goodbye, and Anna had not been the same since. She thought about little else. Now when she showed up at her job at the post office, she remained quiet, not speaking to her coworkers about Mimi. On occasion she overheard people making references to her "traitor" son. It hurt. She hoped he was okay in America, but did not understand the move because he had things going for him here in Cuba. He had a successful baseball career, friends and family. Why did he leave it all behind? On one level, Anna understood Mimi's desire to live in America.

There was freedom and unlimited potential, but it was so painful not to see him. Anna sighed. At least she and Manny were now able to speak to Mimi by telephone on a more regular basis. And the money they were receiving was very helpful.

It was late afternoon when Anna started cooking dinner. Manny stood at the window, observing the crowded street outside. He sorely missed his big brother and idol, but he was proud of Mimi for leaving. He spent his days trying to dig up all possible information about Mimi's career.

It didn't take long before he spotted the unmarked car parked discreetly down the street. "Looks like they have some new ones today." Sometimes Anna and Manny saw armed security guards roaming outside their house. The police would harass, even stop and frisk Manny right in front of their home.

"Why do they bother?" Anna expressed.

Manny sat down at the table when they heard a rap on their door so harsh that it almost knocked the door from its hinges. Anna wiped her hands on her apron and opened the door. Two tough-looking Cuban security officers stood on the other side. One was almost six feet tall with broad shoulders. He stared at her with his coal black eyes. She couldn't see a shred of kindness in him. The second man was smaller and more slender than his partner. He flashed a smile, but it was not a friendly one. Anna didn't trust him. *A shark might have such a smile before he clamps his teeth into you.*

"Mi hombre es Major Adaso," the tall man said. He briskly walked into the house, not waiting to be invited. His boots pounded harshly on the wooden floor.

Manny stood. "Que deseas? What do you want?"

"Ustedes dos pueden sentarse. Sit down," said the Major.

Manny did not like being ordered around in his own house, but he also knew he was powerless in the face of the state security police, the Cuban Gestapo. Both he and his mother eased down onto the couch. The major and his colleague remained standing.

"We want to know about the latest call with your son," said the major. "Did he mention who he first contacted about leaving, or talk about the escape at all?"

The second officer chimed in, "You realize that providing information will help you in the eyes of the Cuban government. If you cooperate, you will benefit. Otherwise, who knows?"

Manny was frustrated with this routine, and it showed in his response. "We knew nothing."

"To hell you knew nothing! He left here without telling you anything about his plans? He left his mother and brother in the dark? You expect us to believe that?"

Manny grabbed his mother's hand. It was twitching and Manny could feel the sweat on her palm. He took a deep breath and told himself not to get angry. "Major, I assume this is not the first time you have investigated the family of a defector. You should know by now that almost all escapees do not tell their families of their plans. If they did, the family would face reprisals. Mimi knew that and made the calculated decision to tell us nothing. Believe me, I wish I knew more, but I do not."

"And you, senora?" the major snarled, almost growling instead of speaking.

Anna shook her head, "Mimi no me dojo nada."

The officers looked around the apartment, inspecting closets and even rummaging through drawers. They were not careful in their search. They tossed items out of their way, slamming them onto the walls. They pulled drawers out from a desk. They emptied the contents on a bed and dropped the drawers on the floor. Finally, in disgust, the major turned back to them. "If you are withholding information, you will be charged as an accessory and your careers will be over."

Letting the threat linger, the officers left.

Anna was shaking. She got up and walked into the bedroom. She had to clean off items the security men threw on the bed before she could lie down.

"Damn them!" Manny cursed the two officers under his breath, wishing they would burn in hell.

CHAPTER 15

On Saturday Mimi arrived at the ballpark at 2:00 p.m. for a 6:00 p.m. game. He quietly put in his work lifting weights followed by extensive stretching. Working out and playing baseball were antidotes for his depression and loneliness. He was getting ready for batting practice when his two Hispanic teammates, Hector Villa of Venezuela and Benito Aya of Puerto Rico, approached. It had been obvious to them that Mimi had been struggling and more subdued than usual.

"*Que pasa*, Mimi. You okay?" inquired Hector.

Mimi nodded.

Benny insisted, "After the game tonight, the three of us should go out for some dinner and do some partying."

Mimi did not respond.

"Come on, man," said Benny. "All you do is sit at home. You can't just eat, sleep, and play baseball."

Mimi shrugged. "Perhaps it is a good idea."

"All right, then!" said Benny.

Mimi again went 0 for 4 with two more strikeouts, and committed an error overthrowing third base, which led to a run.

It wasn't only Mimi that struggled that night. The Tampa Yankees got skunked 5 to 0.

Mimi took his time showering. He tried to put the game behind him and looked forward to a night out as he got dressed in jeans and a cashmere blazer.

Benny Aya was a big, some would even say overweight, catcher with a charismatic personality. He grew up in Bayamon, Puerto Rico, and was a twenty-eighth round pick who could really play defense behind the plate. He just couldn't hit. Managers, coaches, and scouts loved him because of how much he enjoyed working with pitchers. He called a great game. He could block balls in the dirt, throw out base runners, and do all those other things that catchers do that go unappreciated. Unlike most players, Benny would rather play defense than hit. Just the other day, Mimi saw him before the game with one of the coaches practicing for nearly an hour blocking pitches in the dirt. When he finally missed one, he punished himself by insisting the coach throw fifteen more minutes worth of pitches in the dirt.

Hector Villa, a middle infielder from Venezuela, was not as outgoing as Benny, but was also a great defender who could really run. Neither Benny nor Hector would be considered major league prospects unless they figured out a way to significantly improve their hitting.

At 10:00 p.m., Benny, Hector and Mimi left the clubhouse together and got into Benny's white Escalade. They headed to Habana Cafe and Lounge. It was a Latin restaurant and nightclub outside of Tampa. Benny and Hector frequented it quite often.

As the three of them got out of the car and headed across the street, Benny put an arm around Mimi's shoulder and gave him a friendly shake. "What you need, my brother, is some good old-fashioned rice and beans with a dash of salsa music washed down by more than a few shots of tequila."

They walked into a crowded Habana Cafe with very lively music playing. The scantily dressed hostess recognized Benny and Hector and escorted them to a table where a very pretty waitress was waiting to greet them.

"*Que pasa,* Lola," said Benny, as he hugged her, and then introduced her to Mimi. "Please say hello to Ms. Lola Rosario."

"Nice to meet you," said Mimi.

It took Mimi a second to place her, but then it him. Lola was the girl he saw last week in the outfield. Mimi took another look. It was definitely her, and the sly smile she gave Mimi confirmed it. Suddenly, he felt nervous. He began to sweat. He had been hoping that he would see her again and now that she was standing right in front of him, he had no idea what to say, so he remained silent.

Benny ordered food for the table. First, a round of tequila shots followed by plenty of rice and beans were ordered, with steak, chicken, and fish. "We want some food that has some hits in it!" exclaimed Benny.

Benny could see Mimi staring at Lola as she left the table. "She looks a bit like J-Lo, don't you think?" laughed Benny. "Only better."

When the drinks arrived, Hector made a toast to his amigos. He held his glass high, "To Mimi's inevitable rise to the big leagues. *Salud!*"

Mimi kept watching Lola as she served other tables. *What a smile. What grace. What class.* He just needed the nerve to speak to her so he threw down another shot of tequila. He took one more shot and looked for his opening. He saw Lola talking to the bartender when Mimi stood and approached the bar.

"Hi," he blurted.

"How ya doing, Mimi." She flashed her beautiful smile. "I was hoping you were going to come up and talk to me."

He was already on cloud nine.

"So I hear Tampa is just a pit stop for you on the way to New York," she asked. "Is that true?"

"Hopefully," said Mimi.

The bartender gave her a couple of drinks for her to take to a table.

Sensing his window was closing, Mimi asked, "Would you like to get together when you're done with work tonight?"

"Wait here a minute." She took the drinks over to the customers waiting at a nearby table. On her way back, she grabbed a napkin from the bar and discreetly jotted her number down. "I work too late tonight but definitely another time. Here's my cell. Call me."

Mimi returned to Benny and Hector feeling pretty good about himself. The three continued to celebrate with plenty of food and drinks.

When another round of drinks arrived, Mimi was the one who raised his class first. "I want to thank you guys for getting me out and bringing me here. This is the best time I've had and the best meal I've had since I arrived in Tampa."

The three toasted to that.

At home that night, Mimi was finally able to think of something besides how lost he felt. Images of Lola danced inside his head as he lay down. It was late, but he still picked up the phone to call Willie.

"Sounds like you had a good time tonight," said Willie

Mimi talked for the next twenty minutes, but not a word was said about baseball. Nothing about the game or Mimi's recent struggles on the field. It was all about their night out. "I even met a girl," he added.

"Interesting," said Willie.

"And she's beautiful."

During the game the next day, with the sun blazing in the sky and the temperature close to a hundred degrees, Mimi came to the plate in the first inning with a man on second base. The Daytona Cubs' pitcher tried to fire an inside fastball past Mimi. The pitcher was aware that Mimi had been struggling and thought his reaction time would be a little slow. It turned out that Mimi's timing was perfect. The crack of the bat caused a jolt throughout the stadium. Many in the crowd stood up as they watched the ball clear the left field fence and bounce on a small green mound far in the distance.

Mimi's manager smiled and spit as he watched the ball sail away. "Does this mean his slump is over?" he asked one of his coaches.

That day Mimi went 3 for 4, including a home run in a victory for the Yankees. The next day Mimi went 2 for 2, with two walks, two stolen bases, and an amazing catch in center field that took away a sure double. He was back.

On the bus ride to Viera, the players were in an upbeat, lively mood. When Mimi arrived in his hotel room, he decided it was time to make his move and call Lola. He dug the napkin with her number out of his pocket and dialed. It went to voicemail. Damn. When he heard the beep, he stuttered. "Hi Lola, this is Mimi Mijares. Right now I'm in Viera after a two-day trip to St. Lucie where I played well. My team won and now I hope you will keep my hot streak going by agreeing to go out with me when I get back to Tampa on Thursday. What do you think?"

After hanging up, Mimi slapped his forehead. *Continue my hot streak? Am I in junior high? Try some sophistication.* In an attempt to forget about the message, he got to work unpacking his clothes. He wasn't even done when the phone rang. It was Lola. He took a deep breath. He told himself to calm down and then he answered. He couldn't remember the last time he was so nervous, but Lola quickly put him at ease.

"How's my handsome Cuban doing?" she asked.

Mimi relaxed and they talked for a half hour. Before getting off the phone, they made plans for Mimi to pick Lola up after work next Thursday and get a drink together.

For the rest of the road trip, all Mimi could think about was Lola. When Thursday night rolled around, Mimi showed up at the restaurant in his white Escalade at exactly 11:00 p.m. Lola was already outside waiting. They drove to a club a mile down the road. Unlike Habana Cafe and Lounge, this place was quiet with live jazz music.

The couple sat down in a cozy booth and ordered drinks and steak dinners. When the drinks came, Mimi and Lola raised their glasses in a toast. "Salud," said Mimi. In Cuba, typically Mimi spent a lot more time on the baseball field than he did courting women. He was a bit reserved by nature. Lola was not. She carried the conversation until he had his second drink.

"So you like baseball?" he asked.

"I used to go to Marlins games with my dad. They won the World Series in '97, but when all the good players left to make more money in free agency, my dad was ticked off so the next year we didn't go to any games. And when the team didn't sign Moises Alou, Edgar Renteria, and Rob Nenn, Dad went nuts."

"You do know baseball."

"Dad lived and breathed it. So did I. I still can picture Renteria getting that winning hit up the middle to win the series."

Not only is she beautiful, but she likes and talks baseball. Mimi didn't want this night to end. He wanted to keep her talking. "Well it's not the World Series, but would you like to come to my game tomorrow night? I'll leave you tickets."

"Can I bring my friend Carol?"

"I'll leave two tickets in your name. You can pick them up at Will Call. Game starts at seven."

After eating delicious beef and rice dinners, they finished off another round of drinks. Lola asked Mimi about his life in Cuba, and for the first time that day, his mood soured. He shook his head.

"I don't like to talk about Cuba. There are too many bad memories. All I can say is that I miss my mother and brother. I'm going to see if I can bring them to the United States." Mimi shrugged. "Let's talk about something else."

Lola put her hand on his, and smiled. "I apologize. I just want to get to know you better."

"Thanks for understanding."

"How many more games left this season?" she asked, changing the subject.

"Twenty. Then playoffs. When this season is over, I'll get a couple of weeks off and then get ready for the Arizona Fall League in October. I don't wanna jinx it, but there are rumors that I might be called up to the major leagues in September. That means I get to play in Yankee Stadium." Mimi found himself rambling. "But tell me about you. How come you aren't married with a couple of kids?"

"I was married. For five years. That didn't work out. My divorce became final six months ago." Lola took a healthy gulp from her drink.

"What happened?" asked Mimi. "Tell me about it."

No response. Now it was Mimi's turn to say something soothing, "I apologize. I just wanted to get to know you better."

They both laughed. Mimi ordered another round of drinks, and they enjoyed the music. They didn't speak for several minutes, but Lola scooted over next to him and put her hand in his. After baseball, music was Mimi's second passion, especially jazz. The piano player spoke softly into the microphone and what he said brought a smile to Mimi's face. "The next two numbers are a tribute to the great Dizzy Gillespie and Arturo Sandoval. Con Alma and Salt Peanuts. I hope you enjoy."

Mimi closed his eyes and allowed his mind and soul to become part of the music. He thought about the many piano lessons he received from his aunt back in Cuba. He played regularly for several years until baseball took over his life. When the song ended, Mimi opened his eyes. The band went on break. He turned to Lola. "Let's take a walk."

As they exited the restaurant arm in arm, Lola slyly asked, "Would you like my company tonight or would you rather spend another night alone?"

Mimi was somewhat taken aback by her aggressiveness. A girl would never say that back home in Cuba on the first date, but he smiled and said, "Sure."

That night back at his apartment Mimi was quite nervous as he attempted small talk, but quickly realized how little they knew about each other. Lola, on the other hand, did not seem nervous at all as she cuddled up to Mimi on the couch. She moved closer and slowly began to unbutton his shirt. Mimi could smell her perfume. Lola looked into his eyes as she gently kissed him on the lips. Mimi was all too happy to let her be in control. She took his hand and led him into the bedroom. Although reserved and not a ladies man, Mimi was a handsome baseball player who certainly did not lack for feminine companionship when he wanted it back in Cuba. Still, he had never met a woman like Lola.

That night, Mimi slept better than he had in weeks. In the morning, they went at each other again, after which Lola hurriedly dressed herself, kissed him, and left rather quickly.

"See you tonight at the game," she said.

That night after the game, Lola came home with Mimi and ended up staying over the next five nights.

It wasn't until Mimi checked his e-mail and saw a message from Willie that he realized that he hadn't spoken to his agent in almost a week. Willie said that they needed to go over his career and financial planning. He told Mimi that he would be in Tampa at the end of the week and suggested they meet up after his Saturday night game.

CHAPTER 16

For the third consecutive evening, Carol picked up Lola at Mimi's apartment and they drove to the ballpark. The two women picked up the tickets at the Will Call window left for them by Mimi and proceeded to the family section in the stands behind home plate.

Lola quickly learned that this section was quite a scene. This was where players' wives, girlfriends, fiancées, friends, relatives, and other associates sat to enjoy the game. Sometimes players also left tickets for business contacts. They often used tickets as a barter system so that they could have use of a car from a dealer, get work done at their apartment, or free meals at restaurants.

Lola noticed that many of the girlfriends and wives were not there to watch the game at all, but rather to be part of a social scene. In the family section, women often dressed more like they were going to a nightclub than a baseball game. Gossip and rumors were endless. Lola and Carol grew to enjoy the scene, sometimes mocking but also participating in the frivolous activities. Discussions ranged from how much money this one was making to who was cheating on who and how much of a signing bonus each player received. Rumors were constantly circulating about who was being moved up to AA, AAA, or the major leagues. Some of these women sounded like they were speaking with authority, despite not really knowing what they were talking about.

The ringleader of the family section was clearly Cindy Cunningham, former high school sweetheart and fiancée of pitcher Billy Cunningham. Cindy was a very pretty Texas girl. Her hair, makeup, and lipstick were just perfect as she relished being the center of attention and holding court in the family section. It also looked like she had spent a good portion of Billy's signing bonus on jewelry and clothes.

Alexander Harte, president of Premier Sports Agency out of Houston, Texas, walked down the aisle just above the family section. Harte was handsome and in his midforties, with flowing blond hair. He maintained a casual yet impeccable appearance. Billy was one of Alex's prized clients, so Alex flew into town to watch him pitch. Cindy caught Harte's eye and he quickly made his way over to join her. "Cindy, looking great as always. I'm expecting a good outing from Billy. He could find himself moving up to AA soon. From there the big leagues are a phone call away."

Cindy crossed her fingers for good luck, and the two hugged. They chatted for a few minutes. Harte maneuvered his way over to the next section where he said hello to the girlfriend and the brother of Carl Hunt, another Harte client, who was the right fielder for the Ft. Myers Twins. Today Hunt would compete against Billy and the Tampa Yankees. The same year that Alex negotiated the $3.75 million signing bonus for Billy, he also negotiated a $2 million signing bonus for Carl.

From four rows behind, Lola carefully watched Harte. "Check this guy out," Lola whispered to Carol. What Lola did not know was that Harte was currently asking Cindy if she could provide an introduction to Mimi Mijares via Lola.

In the first inning, the Ft. Myers club went down one-two-three as Billy struck out the first two batters and retired the third on an easy fly ball to Mimi in center field. Mimi was the third hitter to bat in the bottom of the first inning, and following a walk to Eddie Ring, he hit a long home run, deep into the right field seats to give Tampa a 2-0 lead.

Lola stood and cheered wildly. She exchanged high fives with a few of the other nearby fans. When the first inning ended, Lola went to the restroom. On the way back to her seat, Cindy and Alex approached her in the aisle. "That was quite a hit by your man," Cindy exclaimed. "Whatever you're doing, keep doing it."

"I'll try my best," said Lola, loving the attention.

"Anyway, I would like you to meet Alex Harte. He happens to be our agent and very much wanted to meet you."

"Nice to meet you," responded Lola.

"The pleasure is mine," said Alex. "Mimi is playing great baseball and should have a great future."

The three engaged in a little more small talk before Harte had to excuse himself. "Listen, I have to go see someone in the office, but when I'm done I would love to sit down with you for a brief chat. Would that be all right?"

"I guess that would be okay," said Lola, who suddenly realized that she could assert some influence.

The pitchers dominated the next couple of innings, which allowed most of those in the family section to concentrate on gossip. Mimi came to bat in the bottom of the third inning and was walked on four pitches.

"I guess they're afraid of him now," said Harte as he walked down the aisle and approached Lola. "Do you mind if I sit here for a few minutes?"

"Please do. This is my friend, Carol."

"So nice to meet you," said a smiling Carol, as she extended her hand.

After a brief chat about the weather, Harte got right to the point. "Listen, Lola, at your convenience I would love to have a meeting with you and Mimi. I will happily fly you guys to my office in Houston or meet you anywhere, anytime in Florida. Whatever fits your schedule. Very casual. No obligations whatsoever. I would like you to hear about what our company has to offer in terms of representing your interests. I'm sorry to say this, but Mimi's current agent has already cost him millions of dollars."

That got Lola's attention. "I don't know about that, but I do know Willie has been a good friend to Mimi."

"Maybe he has, but sometimes that's part of the problem. Having a friend in charge of your business affairs may not be the best idea. Would you have someone perform heart surgery on you because he's a friend? Of course not. And you should consider your career and financial health serious stuff as well. Don't hire someone because he's a friend, but rather hire someone with experience and a track record of success. Do you realize that all Mimi had to do was establish residency in the Dominican Republic, Mexico, or

Costa Rica, which is relatively easy to do, and he could have been a free agent and not subject to the amateur draft. That way he could have negotiated with all the teams instead of just one. I would like to have a chance to explain the whole process to you and Mimi and show you how and why the signing bonus he received was about one-third or one-fourth of what he should have received."

Lola shook her head. "Are you sure about that?"

"Now is not the time or place to get into any of this. How about you give me your number and we can chat in a couple of days?"

That night Lola couldn't get the conversation with Harte out of her head. He called her the very next day when she was on break from work. Much to her surprise, he also started pitching her. "Our company works with some modeling agencies and I have no doubt we could get you some work in that area if you're interested. There are great advertising opportunities for bilingual women. Especially those with your striking good looks."

Lola's interest was piqued, but she tried not to let on so she ended the call and promised to continue their conversation later. The next day, she received in the mail a picture of the 1997 Florida Marlins with autographs from many of the players on that club. She had no idea how Alex Harte even knew about her connection to the Marlins.

CHAPTER 17

On Saturday afternoons, Willie regularly joined his grandfather at the Little Havana Activity Center while he played Cuban canasta with his close friends. All of Ivan's friends loved Willie because he would always joke with them and talk baseball, but this Saturday was different. His mind was on Mimi. Their recent telephone conversations had been different. Mimi seemed distant. Maybe it was due to his recent slump. Willie just wanted to get to Tampa and hopefully put things in perspective to help Mimi.

When the card game ended and Ivan's friends got up for a quick break, Ivan cut right to the chase with Willie, "What's on your mind?"

"Mimi. He's struggling, even seems depressed."

"Of course, he's struggling mentally. You have no idea. You may have studied Cuban history, but Mimi, like me, has lived it. He's seen Fidel in action firsthand. He's seen the sadness of the people who have no aspirations. He's seen the living conditions, buildings in ruins, hopelessness. Now he's here while his mother and brother are there. What do you expect?" Normally Ivan usually didn't want to talk about Cuba, but right now he couldn't stop. He gestured with his hands as he continued.

"Ever since 1959, Castro's revolution brought Cuba into direct conflict with the United States. America imposed an economic embargo in order to undermine the new regime. No more American business transactions. Policies were put into place that seriously damaged the Cuban economy. It didn't take long for misery and poverty to consume much of the population. Thereafter, the Soviet Union became Cuba's largest trade partner providing critical subsidies. Of course America did not like that."

Willie heard enough for now, hugged his grandfather, and left.

As usual, Willie did not obey the speed limit as he drove his Corvette on Interstate 4 toward Tampa Stadium. It was nearly 10:30 p.m. Saturday night when he pulled into the players' parking lot. The game had ended an hour ago with a Yankee victory. Mimi got three hits and was locked in at home plate once again. His batting average was back up to .328.

Willie walked to the clubhouse exit where the players leave after the game. There were already about twenty people gathered in the area. Willie phoned his wife and checked his e-mails while waiting for Mimi. He happened to catch a glance of a very pretty girl about fifteen feet away, but had no idea this was the girl Mimi had spoken about in their recent telephone conversations.

Mimi was one of the first players to exit the clubhouse. He had a big smile on his face as he approached Lola and gave her a kiss. Then he noticed Willie so he walked over and gave him a hug. "Willie, I want you to meet Lola."

"So very nice to meet you," she said extending her hand. "I've heard so much about you. This is my friend, Carol."

Willie nodded and shook both of their hands. "Nice to meet you as well."

"Let's go out, the four of us, and get to know each other," laughed Mimi, awkwardly.

It did not take long for Willie to realize that this was not going to be the serious meeting he was hoping for dealing with career and financial matters. Willie wanted to feel good that Mimi was playing much better and happy about this new relationship, yet something did not seem right. The usually shy and reserved Mimi was a little full of himself. Lola was all over Mimi, holding his arm and kissing his cheek as the four of them proceeded to their respective cars. Willie was getting the idea that he may no longer be Mimi's number one go-to confidant. He knew that professional athletes were often superstitious beings. Mimi was hitting nearly .400 since Lola came into the picture. Everyone was telling him how well he was performing. It was natural for him to think of Lola as his good luck charm, and there was no way that Willie could compete with that.

The four of them grabbed a bite to eat at a local Mexican restaurant. Mimi and Lola were all over each other, leaving Willie and Carol to engage in awkward conversation. At one point, Willie thought Carol was coming on to him and that was the last thing he needed. Finally, Willie looked at Mimi, and said, "I get that you are up for a little celebrating, but I was hoping to talk to you. There's a lot that we need to go over."

"Definitely, let's do it," responded Mimi, pouring himself another margarita from the pitcher. "We'll go back to our apartment."

The fact that he said "our" apartment did not go unnoticed by Willie. Mimi and Lola had been together less than two weeks and already it was "our apartment."

After dinner, Carol went home while the others went to Mimi's apartment. Willie and Mimi sat at a small table in the living room while Lola went into the bedroom. Willie pulled out some financial statements from his briefcase that summarized Mimi's investment portfolio. Willie explained that Mimi's signing bonus was distributed into several conservative no-load mutual funds that overall had not been performing very well lately, but Willie preached the value of staying patient.

"The stock market goes through ups and downs, but these funds provide a balanced approach that will result in solid returns on your investment in the long run."

Mimi appeared disinterested so Willie transitioned the conversation to baseball.

"I'm starting to figure out how pitchers are going after me," said Mimi. "Especially the good ones. Lately a lot of these guys are sort of pitching me backwards. Breaking balls behind in the count. First pitch breaking ball. In Cuba, if the count is 2-0 or 3-1, you know a fastball is coming."

Mimi and Willie were now relaxing. They were both more comfortable while talking baseball. "Here in the States, quality pitchers quickly figure out what the hitter's strengths and weaknesses are and make adjustments as to how to attack certain hitters. Once it gets in the scouting reports, the word gets out fast. It's more about command of the baseball than it is how hard you can throw. Once the pitchers make adjustments, it's up to the hitters to make their adjustments. And that process never ends. It's a game of who wins the battle of adjustments." Willie laughed. "Is the hitting coach helping you?"

"A little bit. He's getting me to understand the hitting zone. He keeps saying pitchers know who is overly aggressive and who is a patient hitter. If you are too aggressive, then almost every pitch will be thrown off the plate and outside the strike zone. They want to entice you to swing at a pitchers' pitch. Once scouting reports indicate that I'm a disciplined hitter, I will get better pitches to hit."

"Yea, take your walks," added Willie. "If pitchers can get hitters to swing at pitches four to six inches off the plate, their batting averages will be well under .250."

Mimi threw down another shot of tequila. Both Mimi and Willie were quite animated as they talked about the game they loved, playing catch right there in the living room.

"Mimi, I suggest you keep a book on each pitcher you face."

"A book?"

"Documenting which pitches they throw and in what situations. Does he have a quality breaking ball with the confidence to throw it even when he is behind in the count? Is he a nibbler or does he challenge hitters with fastballs right in the zone? Is his approach to get ahead in the count by throwing a first-pitch fastball for a strike? What is the difference in how he goes after hitters at the top and bottom of the order as compared to the run producers in the middle of the lineup? Does he pitch differently as the game goes on so that he might attack you one way early in the game, but differently in the late innings?"

"A couple of the really good pitchers I faced set me up by pitching me a certain way in my first two at bats, but when the game was on the line, late in the game they adjusted their game plan."

"See? You're picking up on it already."

"You hear the rumors about me getting called up to the major leagues in September?"

"I actually want to talk to you about that."

Before he could continue, Lola emerged from the bedroom wearing a sexy nightgown and sat on Mimi's lap. Willie frowned as Mimi and Lola kissed and giggled. He knew that this was all he was going to get out of Mimi tonight. Willie could sense that Lola had an agenda, but Mimi seemed happier and more confident than he had been a few weeks earlier. Confidence was a good thing, but so was humility. Ten days ago Mimi was obsessed with the well-being of his brother and mother back in Cuba, but now did not even mention their names. Willie wanted to talk about arranging visa travel to the United States for Manny and Anna, but it never even came up. Willie could only hope that this girl was going to be a positive influence.

It was already past midnight so Willie politely said his goodbyes. He wasn't looking forward to the four-hour drive back to Miami.

After he left, Lola cuddled in bed with Mimi. "He thinks I'm intruding on his turf."

"Who?" said Mimi, half paying attention.

"Willie. Do you think he's smart enough to represent all your interests? I just hope for your sake he knows what he's doing and has the necessary contacts and influence to help you in every way."

"Why wouldn't he?"

"I heard what he said about your investments not doing so well. And I don't know how the baseball business works, but maybe he should be talking with the Yankees about calling you up to the major leagues in September. I know how much that would mean to you. It seems to me they owe that to you for how well you're playing. It would also be a good public relations move for them."

"Willie is my friend," responded Mimi. "I would not be here if it wasn't for him."

"Yesterday at the ballpark an agent named Alex Harte came up and spoke to me. Cindy Cunningham made the introduction."

"You talked to another agent about me?"

"I didn't. He brought it up. He represents Billy as well as many others throughout the major and minor leagues. He wants to meet."

"What did you say?" snapped Mimi. "I hope you told him I have an agent and I'm not interested."

"Yes, I told him you have an agent, but he said Willie is not getting you what you deserve. Maybe he is, maybe he's not. I don't know, but you have nothing to lose by just meeting with him."

Lola turned over and ran her fingers down Mimi's chest. Slowly they moved into a cozy embrace in bed.

CHAPTER 18

Manager Tommy Harlan called Mimi into his office before the game on Monday night. It was the last week of August. Coach Yo Miranda was there as well just in case any translation was necessary, although by this time Mimi was quite able to comprehend English.

"You're playing very good baseball," said Tommy. "You're putting up good numbers. Doing everything we ask and expect. Your future is bright, but I want to give you a heads-up that the Yankee front office has decided not to call you up to the majors in September."

Mimi could feel all the air get sucked out of the room. This was a strange feeling for him because he wasn't used to being overlooked like this. Yo avoided eye contact, but Tommy knew exactly what to say to keep Mimi focused.

"It's important that you understand the decision is not a negative reflection on you at all. This is not a punishment. They are only calling up four extra players, two pitchers and two position players. The two position players have prior major league experience. The big club is in a tight pennant race and only wants to call up players they need to help win the division. This is not a season in which numerous September call-ups are brought on to see what they can do for the future. If the situation were different, you'd probably get a call-up to see what you could do. Right now, they think it's best you finish up here and get ready for the Arizona Fall League."

"I guess I can use the rest," added Mimi, struggling to find a positive spin.

"You will be invited to major league camp next spring training. Once you make the jump, we want you to stay there and have success. We don't want you to be one of those players who keep going back and forth."

Mimi barely heard anything after learning he wouldn't be called up. Coach Miranda periodically interjected some Spanish into the conversation, but it was not needed. Mimi heard the message in two languages and was disappointed in both. Even though he was not expecting to get to the major leagues this season, he was surprised at how disappointed he felt to get the news. He tried not to think about the rumors and all the people who had told him he was getting to the "show," but he couldn't help but get caught up in the hype.

"Just finish strong down here," Tommy went on. "Continue to give a good impression to the major league staff."

***

About the same time as Mimi was having a meeting with his manager, Lola received a phone call from Alexander Harte. "Sorry about Mimi not getting the big league call-up."

"Really?" said Lola. She had no idea how Alex found this news out so quickly.

"It's unbelievable after what he's done. And he's thirty years old. What are they waiting for? It would be a great public relations move for the Yankees, not to mention that he could help them in their push for the pennant. I don't get it. I don't know if his agent tried to put the pressure on the front office, but I assure you they would have gotten an earful from me. Willie undoubtedly has other things on his mind."

"What are you talking about?"

"I heard from a reliable source that some news will be coming out of Miami's United States Attorney's office about legal troubles for Willie."

Lola's mind raced after she hung up with Harte. She didn't get a chance to speak with Mimi before the game, but spent the entire time in the stands mulling over what she learned from Harte.

The game that night did not go so well. Mimi took the collar, going 0 for 4. He did hit the ball hard twice, but the team lost 7 to 2. Lola chatted with some of the wives before she made her way to the parking lot to meet with Mimi. Once she saw him walk out of the locker room, she could see that he was not in a very good mood. She didn't say a word. She just took his hand and walked with him across the lot. Mimi finally broke the silence when they reached his car. "I'm not going to the big leagues—"

"I know."

"How could you possibly know? Tommy said they haven't announced anything yet about September call-ups."

"That agent Alex Harte called. This guy has his ear to the ground. He seems to know everything that's going on in the business. And he also had some negative things to say about Willie."

"Like what?"

"He believes a more experienced agent might have made a difference. He said that Willie has other things on his mind, whatever that means, but some sort of news will be coming out of Miami that may explain it."

"What news? He didn't tell me anything?"

"I have no idea, but I think Willie may be in some sort of trouble with the law."

At home that night, Mimi listened as Lola continued her verbal assault on Willie.

"I realize he's been your friend, but does that mean he should be in charge of your financial and career management?"

"I'm not just going to dump him."

"Wake up! Your investment portfolio is going down in value. You didn't get called up to the big leagues, and you did deserve a call-up. You received a signing bonus significantly below what you should have received. It makes me wonder." Lola could tell that she was starting to get through to Mimi so she kept her foot on the gas. "I hear stuff at the ballpark about all the merchandise, equipment, and even endorsement opportunities agents are getting their players. Shoes, bats, clothes, all kinds of things—"

"It's not about that stuff —"

"You have an entire fan club in the bleachers! Maybe your agent missed an opportunity to market something there."

"So what do you want me to do?"

"Meet with Alex. You might learn something."

"I know nothing about this guy?"

"Mimi, I hate to say this, but sometimes here in the United States people in power, such as owners of baseball teams, give more credibility to their own kind, white businessmen, than they do to someone like Willie."

Mimi got up and made himself a drink. "The season here is over in a couple of weeks. I'll meet with him then, before I leave for Arizona."

A smile of self-satisfaction came over Lola's face as she slowly advanced toward Mimi. She unbuttoned his shirt and caressed his chest. She started working her way down. It took about thirty seconds for a hint of a smile to appear on Mimi's face.

"I think that's a very good plan," said Lola.

CHAPTER 19

The following Monday, Assistant United States Attorney Charlie Mann and Assistant Secretary of Homeland Security Teri Mills issued the following joint press release:

"Today the federal grand jury in Dade County issued a federal indictment against Guillermo 'Willie' Santos, charging multiple violations of United States Code 8 USC Section 1324 . . . smuggling into the United States Cuban baseball players knowing that such aliens had not received prior official authorization to enter the United States, with the purpose of obtaining commercial advantage or private financial gain in violation of 8 USC #1324 and to conceal, harbor, or shield from detection such aliens for the purpose of financial gain also in violation of 18 USC Section 371."

The statement was signed by both the Assistant United States Attorney and the Assistant Secretary of Homeland Security. Mimi watched ESPN Deportes in shock as Ms. Mills responded to a question by a reporter. "This case involves a Miami sports agent who put the lives of illegal immigrants at risk and sought profit from their labor. His purpose was to enrich himself by smuggling Cuban nationals into the United States."

Mimi was in shock as he tried to digest the story concerning Willie and the criminal charges. It didn't take long for these reports to be all over the internet. Mimi searched to learn more details. One of the articles noted that this was the first time a sports agent had been indicted under these circumstances.

Mimi was not sure what bothered him more, the fact that his friend and agent was under criminal indictment, or that in all their lengthy telephone conversations Willie never thought to say a word about such an investigation. *How could Willie not talk to me about this and just leave me to hear about it in the news?* Mimi picked up the phone and called Willie, who was defensive and irate.

"Listen, Mimi, I'm sorry, but this is the biggest bunch of bullshit ever. Not only is what they're saying not true, but nobody has ever been criminally charged for smuggling athletes into the country. I don't know if it's a political thing, part of the anti-immigration movement, or what. My lawyer is confident that this whole thing will go away. Please don't worry about it. We're going to demand a speedy trial, which puts pressure on the government to turn over its evidence and begin a trial within 120 days."

"How could you not tell me about this investigation?" Mimi incredulously inquired.

"I never thought it would get this far. Something fishy is going on. Cuban ballplayers and Cubans in general have been defecting to the United States for years. That is a larger issue about a great deal more than me, Willie Santos. Let me ask you, have any investigators contacted you for an interview?"

"No."

"What does that tell you? They're just shooting from the hip. If they were really being thorough about a serious investigation, they would have tried to interview you. By the way, if anybody does contact you about this, let me know."

Now Mimi was even more upset due to the prospect of being dragged into this mess. He pictured someone from the FBI knocking at his door any moment. Just what he needed.

"Mimi, just keep doing your thing, don't worry. Nothing changes between us. I'll take care of this matter. It will disappear."

Mimi was not so sure about that, but he did his best to put it out of his mind so he could finish strong. The Florida State League playoffs ended quickly for the Yankees. The first round was a best of three, and the Tampa Yankees lost the first two games 8 to 5 and 4 to 3. That was all it took. They were done. Mimi did his part trying to keep the season alive by producing three hits in each game, including a homer, three RBIs, and two stolen bases. Billy Cunningham pitched seven strong innings in the second game and left with a 3-to-1 lead, but the bullpen failed.

Mimi was now ready to take a break from baseball until the Arizona Fall League started in six weeks. He was planning on a few days of doing nothing baseball related, after which he would challenge himself to an intense workout schedule to get stronger and some batting practice to stay sharp.

The latest publication of *Baseball America* came out a day later and ranked Mimi as the number two prospect in the Yankee organization and the number fifteen prospect in all of baseball. That meant a great deal of attention was about to come his way, including calls from various agents, investment advisors, coaches, scouts, reporters, and others seeking to latch on to his coattails. Mimi was starting to feel pretty good about himself. Everyone was telling him how great he was and Mimi was believing it.

Willie often warned him about getting sucked into the hype and about all the players he had seen lose their edge, change their mental and physical preparation, and fail to progress. “Don’t get too high when things are going well or too low when they are not,” Willie had warned. “Make sure you don’t lose sight of what it takes to be a major league baseball player. Treat it like a job and grind it out every day.”

While Mimi remembered those words and took that advice seriously, he found his mind and his life gravitating more toward Lola. Her persistence paid off, and Mimi finally agreed to meet with Harte. His office arranged two first-class airplane tickets so Lola and Mimi could fly to Houston. A stretch limousine was waiting at the airport when they arrived and drove them over to the offices of Premier Sports Agency. Neither Lola nor Mimi had ever ridden in a limousine before; certainly not in a vehicle that had a bar and a television.

The Premier Sports Agency offices were large and decorated beautifully with a mix of fine art and unusual sports memorabilia. Mimi chuckled to himself at the contrast between Willie’s storefront office and this first-class operation. A pretty young female receptionist greeted them and asked them to have a seat in the reception area.

After a few minutes, Alex approached them with a Hispanic man beside him. “Welcome, welcome! I want to introduce my associate, Julio Pinero, who has been with me for ten years. Let us give you a little tour of our offices and introduce you to our staff. How was your flight?"

"It was great," responded Lola. "First class is very, very nice."

As they walked through the offices, Mimi noticed the beautiful view of the city outside the large windows. Alex popped into the offices occupied by agents, attorneys, accountants, marketing people, and the office manager, with whom they had brief introductory chats. They passed by a large conference room. Inside were two men and one woman who were pouring through files, spreadsheets, books, and records. These three individuals did not even look up from their work and no introductions were made.

Mimi was impressed with the efficiency of the office. The men and women did not seem like they wasted a lot of time. They dressed professionally, spoke with courtesy, and certainly seemed knowledgeable, competent, and effective.

Lola, Mimi, Julio, and Alex walked into Alex's magnificent office. It contained a large rectangular desk, telephones, computers, and a big-screen television. There was also an oval-shaped table with four chairs around it, an L-shaped couch, and even a bar in the corner. Mimi checked out the various pictures on the wall of Alex with famous athletes, politicians, and entertainers. Alex was obviously a proud Texas Longhorn. Elaborate, gold frames surrounded his graduation certificates from undergraduate school in 1985 and from law school in 1988.

No one could question the smoothness of Alex's style. With a hint of a Southern drawl, he got directly to the point. "We have been in this business over twenty years and have experience in every issue that impacts players, big, medium, or small. We have relationships with and respect from all thirty baseball organizations. They know they cannot mess with us. We can help you with your career going forward. Nothing against your guy Willie, but he has to operate a different way. He might be a nice guy, but there is no way he can represent all of your interests the way we can. We have lawyers, accountants, and marketing people on staff as well as access to the best training facilities in the world. We know which specialists to send you to if you suffer an injury to a finger, thumb, elbow, knee, or whatever. We understand all of the rights and provisions accorded in the collective bargaining agreement that may affect you, including possible assignments of your contract, options, waivers, moving allowances, injury matters, etc. As I mentioned to Lola in a previous conversation, Willie may be a friend, but the right company to represent you has to be more than a friend."

Julio Pinero intermittently began translating in Spanish. He also gave each of them a fancy brochure describing the company, written in both English and Spanish. It had pictures, graphic designs, and text selling the virtues of Premier Sports Agency, including a list of all their clients, major league and minor league, plus a summary of the various services they provided, which were contract negotiations, legal services, financial planning, state and federal tax preparation, endorsements, media training, post-career planning, and other valuable services. There was also a section promoting some of the significant free agent contracts negotiated as well as arbitration contracts presented by the company over the years. Last but not least, there was a section indicating marketing and endorsement deals they had accomplished.

Mimi took a good look at the brochure and a sly smile came to his face. *There is more to being a baseball player than just swinging the bat.*

As the four of them reviewed these documents page by page, Lola and Mimi occasionally looked at each other, very impressed by the brochure and the presentation. Mimi remained fairly quiet during the meeting, but Lola asked a few questions. Along with the company brochure, Alex handed them certain forms and agreements to review in the event Mimi decided to make a change and designate Premier Sports Agency as his exclusive representative when the telephone rang.

"It's Billy Cunningham," said Alex.

Mimi did not think this call was a coincidence. And it wasn't. After a couple of minutes, Alex put Mimi on the phone with Billy and they had a very pleasant conversation in Spanglish. Billy had a way of getting a laugh out of Mimi. At the end of their conversation, Billy strongly urged Mimi to join "our" company.

"It's all good," Billy liked to say. "I promise you will not regret it."

After some small talk, Alex said goodbye to Billy and turned his attention back to Mimi. "Your limousine is ready to take you to your hotel. Settle in and relax for a while because we have a dinner reservation for 7:00 o'clock. It's a casual steak place with a Latin flavor. A few members of the company will join us, including the gentleman who operates our state-of-the-art workout facility. I must remind you, your flight back to Tampa is at nine tomorrow morning."

The hotel room was an exquisite suite at the Westin Galleria, first class all the way, including a hot tub. As they entered the suite, Lola's eyes lit up. She gave Mimi a long, juicy kiss. That sexy look came over her. They quickly disrobed and made love in the hot tub.

At dinner, Alex continued his assault on Willie. "If he was a lawyer, I would say he committed malpractice by not arranging for you to become a free agent. The dollars he cost you right there are astronomical. By taking a few steps to establish residency, you could have been a free agent eligible to negotiate with all thirty teams instead of being drafted and therefore the property of one team. Inexcusable. Instead of driving right into the United States from Mexico, we would have taken you to this vacation spot right on the beach on the west coast of Mexico where you would have remained until we worked out the logistics with Major League Baseball for you to become a free agent. We have a working relationship with a company in Mexico that would have taken great care of you. By the way, the pork chops are great here, as are the lamb chops and the sea bass. And definitely the mojitos."

Several Premier Sports Agency professionals were at dinner with them and rendered valuable information to Mimi. Elisa Rivera had a few prepared words focusing on bilingual marketing, and Lee Snyder spoke to them about financial planning, investment counseling, and tax preparation. Todd Glick then gave a short presentation describing their connection to various training and rehabilitation facilities.

As the dinner concluded, and they started to leave the restaurant, Alex took Mimi and Lola aside and started rambling about an upcoming sale of his business to a public company conglomerate called Creative Sports Entertainment Media Management Group.

"Those suits you saw in our conference room today were lawyers for Creative Sports Entertainment Media Management Group completing their due diligence for the purchase of our business for $35 million. They are going through all of our books, records, and agreements with clients, preparing the necessary employment agreements, releases, etc."

Mimi wondered whether the consumption of several alcoholic beverages by Alex was contributing to him openly discussing this matter.

"The new company will be able to significantly expand our abilities from a marketing and financial standpoint. They are purchasing other businesses, including, by the way, one that represents models and supermodels." Alex looked at Lola as he made this point. "I see a great future for you guys in the new company. Mimi, you're going to be our number one client in terms of bilingual markets. One of the companies already under the umbrella is the top Spanish-speaking media network and entertainment outlet. There's a lot of synergy going on here that will be to your benefit."

Lola and Mimi said good night to Alex and the others and returned to their hotel for another jump in the hot tub. By the end of the evening, with some further prodding from Lola, Mimi made the decision to switch agents. He came to be convinced that this was all about business and that Alex Harte should be his guy.

The next morning, with the help of Alex, Mimi drafted a termination letter to Willie, basically thanking him for the service he had provided in the past, but indicating that he decided to change his representation for the future. Lola and Mimi were taken to the airport to return to Florida. They certainly enjoyed their first-class return flight to Tampa.

The next day, Mimi thought about ignoring the inevitable telephone call from Willie, but he decided to answer the call. As expected, Willie had a ferocious response. "What are you thinking? I'm here for you and have been here for you in every way. I always will be. You know how important our personal connection is to me. Alex Harte will drop you like a lead balloon as soon as it suits him. He's the ultimate frontrunner."

Alex warned Mimi that Willie would react this way, but Willie wasn't done yet. "I will be there as your friend in good times and in bad. This is a business that is intensely personal in nature. It is not rocket science. No one cares more and will do what is necessary to help you make the adjustments to be successful here in the United States like I will. Period! Look how much time you and I spend together in person and on the telephone discussing everything under the sun. Your ability to get your mind and emotions in the right place is the only way you're going to make it."

When Willie got everything off his chest, Mimi did his best to explain the business aspect of the decision. When he brought up the issue of free agency, Willie could not hold back. "You and I talked about that specific issue at length and you clearly did not want to leave the United States in order to take the necessary steps to establish residency elsewhere. Come on, Mimi! Don't rewrite history here. Not only that, but all you talked about was your dream to play for the Yankees, not become a free agent."

"Willie, I like you as a friend and hope we can remain friends, but this is a decision that I made for my future. I can only hope you understand," pleaded Mimi. That was the suggested quote given to him by Harte as the response to whatever Willie said, but Mimi could tell that Willie was hurt beyond words.

"Something tells me that Lola was behind this," said Willie.

Mimi wouldn't get into the specifics. He quickly got off the phone. He felt bad, but he also felt that his future was in better hands with Harte so he tried to convince himself that he did the right thing even if it didn't feel quite right yet.

Meanwhile, Willie sat behind the desk in his office, staring at the wall. The criminal indictment was serious, and now he began to wonder whether his business would fall apart. He was confident that he could prevail in the legal dispute, but losing Mimi as a client was personal. A friend had stabbed him in the back. Or in the heart. Either way, the wound was bleeding.

Willie leaned back in his chair and wondered whether he should even remain in this crazy business. *I have a degree in economics, excellent people skills, and am bilingual. There are plenty of other jobs I can pursue.* He did not look forward to telling his wife the bad news. There was no logical reason for Mimi to leave him as a client, but that was the way it would apparently go down. This was not the first time this happened in this business, and it certainly would not be the last.

Willie recalled a story relayed to him by an agent he respected very much by the name of Bill Davis. Davis told him about the time he was fired by two players in the same week even though Bill had won two salary arbitration awards for these players. Bill had his own small law practice in Chicago and did not prepare any fancy brochures to pump himself up. He just did his job in a professional, workmanlike manner. However, apparently these two players were so impressed by a dog-and-pony-show put on by some large corporation, which included limousines and women, not to mention payoffs or improper inducements, such as a year's supply of shoes and bats.

Perhaps I should have given Mimi more severe warnings about the parasites in this business. Then again, Willie knew that he had to compete against both that sleazy Alex Harte and Lola. After several hours, Willie lifted himself from the chair and headed home.

"What? Fuck that guy!" Marilyn shouted. A lovely blonde of forty who looked several years younger, Marilyn was normally quite composed, but right now she was outraged. "We've talked about this. Let's face it, some of these ballplayers are idiots! They aren't sophisticated businessmen. They have no clue! They're young, impressionable kids who just happen to have the potential to be worth a lot of money. I understand that companies lose clients in all businesses, but in most other fields at least you're dealing with educated people with some business acumen. In this case, pardon my French, it appears his dick made the decision."

"When a man's brain slips below his waist, there's a problem," replied Willie.

"Don't worry about it. You'll get other clients."

Marilyn kissed Willie on the cheek, and left the room. Willie thought back on the decision to have Mimi go through the draft and take the $600,000 signing bonus from the Yankees. Maybe he should have pushed Mimi to establish residency elsewhere and become a free agent. It is true, there was a path to free agency, which may, and may is a big word here, have led to a more lucrative deal, but this was discussed at length with Mimi, who clearly expressed he wanted no part of such a plan. Mimi knew the truth, but apparently that no longer mattered. Establishing residency required some complicated steps to be taken and carried with it definite risks. The pluses and the security of taking this deal with the Yankees made the most sense. There was no guarantee that he would have received much, if any, more guaranteed money, because of his age and his time away from the game. Moreover, with the Yankees, he signed with a first-class organization that had a plan to develop him quickly to get to the major leagues. Player development, especially for a player like Mimi, was critical, and the Yankees approach gave Mimi his best chance to be successful. The more Willie thought about it, the more he felt they did the right thing no matter what Mr. Alex Harte said. However, that did not make him feel any better as he whispered to himself, "This business sucks," and contemplated his next move.

***

For the next few weeks, Mimi remained in the Tampa area working out and getting ready for the Arizona Fall League, which was scheduled to begin October 20. The league was owned and operated by the thirty major league clubs, each of which sent six of its top prospects to compete in a six-team league. Mimi was feeling very confident from a baseball standpoint despite his disappointment in not getting a September call-up. Each day he showed up at the Yankee complex to work out. Everyone patted him on the back and told him what a great first season he had, and that it was just a matter of time before he'd be a major league star. He both enjoyed the attention and believed the hype. This shy Cuban defector was transforming into a cocky ballplayer.

Willie kept calling, leaving messages where he pleaded for another meeting. Mimi ignored the calls and convinced himself that he had "graduated" from Willie to Alex Harte. He and Lola were developing a friendship with Billy and Cindy Cunningham, who welcomed them to the "major leagues" in terms of his new representation. Eventually, perhaps as an acknowledgment that Willie had been a friend and supporter, Mimi finally agreed to a meeting a couple of days before he was scheduled to leave for Arizona. Lola advised Mimi against such a meeting, arguing that it would only upset him, but he figured the right thing to do was to have this one final meeting before he left town. Mimi was not looking forward to a confrontation, but he owed this to Willie. Along with the guilt Mimi was feeling for betraying Willie were recurring thoughts about his brother and mother back home in Cuba. At times he longed for those long conversations with Willie to get him through difficult mental and emotional times. Meanwhile, Lola was busy upgrading her wardrobe and jewelry, shopping every day. Unlike Mimi, she had been speaking to Alex regularly, hoping to make some progress in her own career of modeling.

Willie and Mimi met at a local Chili's restaurant. Willie sipped a Coke as he talked. "I just don't think you've thought this through. Alex Harte is a slick dude with questionable ethics and not a great deal of business sense. So he wined and dined you. It might look like he has this high-class operation, but he sees his clients as business pawns he can use to get rich off of. They're not his friends. If he could make money selling them out, he will. You and I are friends. I have your best interest at heart, not just as a baseball player, but as a friend."

"I appreciate what you've done for me, Willie. I will never forget it, but Alex has big money and big talent at his agency."

While Mimi did not feel like dealing with this, Willie had a lot to say about things like loyalty, friendship, humility, values, priorities and not falling into traps. Mimi wanted to be polite and respectful, but his true goal was to conclude this meeting and get ready for the move to Arizona. He felt bad about leaving Willie as a client, but he was not about to turn back now.

Willie argued that despite Harte's supposedly first-class operation, his capability in terms of actually helping Mimi in his career was undoubtedly less than that of Willie. Willie knew the collective bargaining rights of the player as well as anyone. "Don't be fooled by the superficial hype. With Alex, you are a small fish in a big pond, and with me, you are a big fish in a small pond. I'm getting locked into the coming Cuban connection to Major League Baseball, short term and long term, which will benefit you. That is the farthest thing from the mind of Mr. Alex Harte. And you can forget having anything close to meaningful conversations that are important to your growth and adjustment to American baseball and American life. This is an intensely personal business. Do not underestimate the value of personal relationships, particularly in your situation. Do you think Alex Harte cares a lick about any of that? Come on, Mimi, it's not too late."

Even though Mimi felt that Willie was making a passionate argument, he was not about to change his mind. The conversation shifted to the pending criminal case against Willie. He explained to Mimi that a pretrial hearing was scheduled in federal court the next Friday and that his attorney had filed a series of pretrial motions to dismiss charges and provide discovery.

"I'm determined to resolve this," stated Willie. "The facts will show that I'm innocent and that the prosecution has engaged in an unfair process against me and my family. I ask you to stand with me."

"I will always consider you my friend, but I can't change my mind again. I've decided to go with Alex."

Willie just shook his head.

The next day Mimi left for Phoenix.

CHAPTER 20

The following Monday morning, Willie had his first appearance in federal court as a defendant. It was supposed to be a routine status call to discuss pretrial discovery and motions. Yet, when Willie arrived at the courthouse he was stunned to see a hundred anti-immigration activists. Some were carrying signs attacking Willie for "smuggling illegals into our country." That hurt. Willie considered himself to be the ultimate American. He was born here, and the son of Cuban refugees. His entire life he sang the praises of the U.S.A. He was proud of the education he received here and of what he accomplished in the greatest country on earth. Not a day went by that he did not communicate his love of America to his family, friends, and acquaintances. But now he was being attacked by some protesters for being un-American.

Willie shook his head. It seemed like everyone was lying about him or betraying him. He was involved in supporting groups that worked for a comprehensive immigration reform bill that would grant a path to citizenship for those currently in this country if they satisfied certain conditions. He also worked tirelessly toward improving the lives of the people of Cuba. He spent years developing relationships with people who were advocating a more humane approach to American diplomacy with Cuba, including easing up on the strict boycott, enhancing the potential for humanitarian aid, and working toward modification of the current travel restrictions between the countries. This often put him at odds with some Cubans in Miami, including his parents, who didn't believe in diplomacy or a relationship between the United States and Cuba as long as Castro was there and changes weren't made. Willie's views regarding Cuban-American policies were probably a minority position in the Cuban communities, although the younger generation was beginning to lean his way.

As Willie walked past these protesters, he wanted to scream out that not only was he born here in America, but each of the Cuban defectors who were the subject of this case were here legally according to United States policy.

One protest sign read, "Go home, Communist," and another read, "Stop Smuggling Illegal Aliens." *Idiots! Morons!*

As they settled into the courtroom, Attorney Rafael Velez sought to calm Willie down. The judge entered and everyone stood as the bailiff called the case. "The United States of America versus Guillermo Santos. Case number 08-3126."

Judge James Shields asked everyone to be seated and addressed the Assistant United States Attorney. "Mr. Mann, have the parties begun to provide discovery to each other?"

"Not yet, Your Honor. No formal requests have been made, but we are prepared today to file our motion for discovery and assume defendant's counsel will do the same. We thought today the court could schedule a time for the filing of any and all pretrial motions, including discovery, and then the parties can begin the process of exchanging discoverable material right away."

"Any response, Mr. Velez?"

"Yes, Your Honor. At this point we would like to file a motion to dismiss the charges and schedule a hearing on the motion. It is our very strong position that once our motion is heard by this court, this case will be over and there will not be any need for further discovery or any other pretrial motions." This comment elicited a chuckle out of Mr. Mann, and Velez directed a sneer toward the prosecution.

"Not only has no such prosecution of a sports agent representing Cuban baseball players ever been attempted in the history of the United States jurisprudence, but we will prove, as a matter of law, that these charges should be dismissed. Moreover, I would ask this court to admonish the prosecution about making public comments over-emphasizing and inaccurately characterizing certain individuals as illegal aliens for the sole purpose of tainting the potential jury pool. That is not what this case is about and Mr. Mann knows it. Each of the ballplayers identified in the indictment is in this country legally. What is going on outside this courtroom right now is a disgrace."

"I have made no such inaccurate comments," responded Mann. "If Mr. Velez thinks he cannot get a fair trial here, he can file a motion for a change of venue."

That was not going to happen since Velez knew he had a better chance with a jury in Miami than he would in a rural, small town.

"Mr. Velez, I will give you fourteen days to file your motion to dismiss with supporting memoranda, and the government has seven days thereafter to file a response," Judge Shields stated. "We will schedule argument on the motion thirty days from now. And Mr. Mann, I won't impose a gag order yet but consider yourself warned. Next case!"

"One more thing, Your Honor," said Mann. "We have requested an increase in bail for the defendant, particularly because he has friends and contacts outside the United States. We believe, therefore, he constitutes a flight risk."

Willie's attorney was about to respond, but Judge Shields waved him off. "The government's request is denied," said the judge. He pounded his gavel to indicate the court session was over.

Arizona, U.S.A.

CHAPTER 21

The Scottsdale Scorpions were up 1-0 on the Salt River Rafters in the bottom of the fourth, but the lackluster inning came to an end when the Rafters clean-up hitter popped up to center field. Instead of running into the dugout, the outfielders remained in their positions while the coach ran out to make a few teaching points with his players.

Mimi watched this all unfold from the bench. He wasn't in the starting lineup today. When the league had begun a few weeks earlier, Mimi was disappointed to learn that he was only going to be in the starting lineup once every three days. The Arizona Fall League was made up of the best prospects in baseball and many of them, no doubt, would find themselves in the major leagues the following season. Each of the six fall league teams were run by major league franchises who decided which players whose development would benefit most by participating in this league. The practices were fairly relaxed. Scouts and agents were everywhere. The games were more instructive than competitive. While the goal in baseball is generally to win the game at hand, that was not the primary focus in this league. Mimi wished someone would have explained that to him before he came. He was one of five outfielders on the team rotating in and out of the lineup.

Mimi bumped fists with his teammates when they finally made their way into the dugout, but he was bored and agitated because he hadn't been able to get into a groove. Twenty games into the season and he still wasn't comfortable at the plate. He was barely hitting above the Mendoza line, .204 to be exact.

At the start of the next inning, Mimi relocated to the back of the dugout where he sat down next to Luis Rivado. Luis was an outstanding young Dominican shortstop who was paid a seven-figure signing bonus and recently identified as the top prospect in the Cincinnati organization according to *Baseball America*. He also spoke very little English, so when Luis was hampered by a hamstring injury that morning, Mimi helped him convey this message to the coaching staff. Luis explained to Mimi he did not have a single Spanish-speaking coach with the Reds—not in Rookie Ball and not on his A-ball club for which he just played this past season.

"For a relatively minimal investment," Mimi said to Luis in Spanish, "the club could have hired one or more retired bilingual infielders to work with you on a daily basis and definitely enhance your development. You know, front office jobs and management positions almost never go to Latinos, but of course it's absurd that on-the-field baseball jobs are not more frequently given to talented bilingual former players. There are hundreds of former major league players from the Dominican Republic, Puerto Rico, Venezuela, and Panama looking for work who could provide significant help to young Latin players. That should be a simple matter."

Luis nodded in agreement.

Mimi couldn't help but think about his conversations with Willie about this and so many other important matters. Now more than ever he longed for his telephone calls with Willie, who would be able to talk him through whatever was going on. He had an urge to call Willie to discuss how he was being used in the Arizona Fall League, and how these top prospect pitchers were pitching to him. He hated starting only one out of every three games and tried to imagine what Willie would say to get his mind right. "Just worry about the things you can control. Work hard. Do what it takes to improve your game, whether you're in the lineup or not. Work on your defensive and offensive fundamentals in practice. During the game, study what the pitchers are doing, especially to the run-producing hitters like yourself. If you aren't in the game, use it to your advantage to mentally prepare for your next opportunity. And stay positive." That's what he would say.

In his head Mimi could hear Willie say those exact words. That was what Willie could do better than anyone, get Mimi's mind right. Now, all these negative thoughts and frustration were not helping him, but Mimi could not call Willie. He felt it would not be the right thing to do under the circumstances. He did try calling Alex Harte, but never got through and instead was transferred to Julio Pinero. Mentally and emotionally, Mimi knew he was struggling again. Thoughts of his brother, mother, and homeland were again starting to overwhelm him. This translated into a return to sleepless nights, bizarre nightmares, and depression.

The game ended a few hours later without Mimi seeing any action. He didn't bother showering. He just wanted to get out of there so he changed out of his clothes and walked back to his modest apartment, but it wasn't much better there. He was now all alone. He and Lola had mutually decided that she would stay behind. It was more Mimi's decision than Lola's. He was looking forward to being away from her for a while. The sex was still good, but the joy in the relationship was dissipating, and he was starting to feel unwanted pressure from her for a commitment.

As Billy Cunningham said to him recently, "She's very pretty, but a little on the high-maintenance side. Mimi, this is your time to play the field a little. You're a hot commodity! You don't even have to do anything. The girls will be coming to you."

Mimi knew that Billy was right. Lola would still call almost every day but was more interested in talking about clothes, jewelry, and gossip. She offered to come to Arizona, but Mimi discouraged it. He wanted to be alone, but where he really wanted to be was back home in Cuba.

Mimi eased himself down behind a small desk in his modest Scottsdale apartment. He smiled as he picked up a book from the table called *The Yankee Century: 100 Years of New York Yankee Baseball*. He started reading. Every time he turned a page, it reinforced his dream to wear the Yankee pinstripes. All the great ones were in the book. Ruth, Gehrig, Dimaggio, Ford, Berra, Mantle. He had read into the 1960s and was awed at the home run battle between Mickey Mantle and Roger Maris in the year Maris broke Ruth's single-season home run record. Maris, more of an introvert than either Ruth or Mantle, was not comfortable with all the publicity. He never adjusted to the spotlight. Mimi had a degree of sympathy for him.

He put down the Yankee book and found himself flipping through the only other book in the room—the Bible. Mimi was not a religious man per se, but he had attended church with his family growing up and often read about the sayings of Jesus. He felt that it was good for the soul. In Cuba, Bibles were forbidden so scraps of pages were hoarded by believers. In America there were endless varieties of the Word and in so many translations. It struck Mimi that what could bring a jail sentence in Cuba was displayed openly in American stores. He always felt that the time spent considering life-and-death questions was beneficial, no matter what religion you practiced. He suddenly realized that the last time he was in a church was his father's funeral and that changed his mood. He closed the book and went to bed.

Mimi arrived at the stadium the following day, excited to learn that he would be in the starting lineup. He quickly got dressed and ran out onto the field to take some fly balls when he noticed a group of young girls shouting his name. Some were apparently members of his fan club, "The Screaming Mimis." He was surprised that his fan club stretched to Arizona. He approached a pretty blond-haired blue-eyed girl, who waved him over.

"Hi, Mimi, I'm Rachel. How you feeling today?"

"Better now," he said with a smile.

"Why don't they play you more often?"

"I was wondering that myself."

"Don't worry about it. You're going to be in the big leagues next year anyway, no matter what happens here."

"I haven't been playing like it lately."

"At least you're still the best-looking guy here."

That caught him off guard. She handed him a piece of paper. "I'm having a little party at my house after the game. Here's my address and phone number."

"I'll try."

After the game, Mimi picked up Luis and off they went to party at Rachel's. Her house was a magnificent home on a golf course with a large swimming pool. At least forty young people were there when Mimi arrived. Drugs and alcohol were flowing. Rachel, obviously a bit inebriated already, offered Mimi some ecstasy, which he declined, but he did happily accept a beer.

The music was blasting and Mimi could not help but notice the many, many attractive girls as they danced, drank, and some swam in the pool. They were very nice to Mimi and quite excited to meet a professional baseball player. He declined an offer to jump in the pool, but did not resist Rachel's subsequent invitation into one of the bedrooms, where they enjoyed each other's near-perfect bodies.

On the way back to his apartment, driving a rented Buick, Mimi noticed he had received two voice messages, one from Lola who, while crying, said how much she missed him and wanted to join him in Arizona. Although he felt bad, he didn't want her in Arizona anytime soon. The second message was from Willie. He wanted to hear about the fall league and expressed hope that his transition to Arizona was going well. Willie concluded his message by inviting Mimi to call him any time if he felt like talking. This was the third time Willie had reached out to him since their last meeting. That was three more than Alex Harte had reached out.

The next day's game was uneventful for Mimi and the team. They won 3-1 and Mimi went 1 for 2 in only four innings of play. He didn't see any action in the outfield except for two routine fly balls before he was replaced and watched the rest of the game from the dugout. Mimi's second at-bat was strong, and even though it was a ground ball single to left, he felt good at the plate and wanted to get a few more chances to see if he could pull himself out of the funk he'd been in since arriving in Arizona.

He was frustrated and wanted to put baseball out of his mind so he welcomed the chance to join Luis and teammate Ramon Casilla at a bar after the game.

CHAPTER 22

At midnight, Luis was in the hospital and Mimi was at the police station.

After waiting alone in the interrogation room for almost an hour, two grouchy looking detectives entered. The Hispanic detective, Diego Blanco, was of medium height with a small scar just above his right eye and about twenty extra pounds hanging over his belt. He joked with his Anglo partner, Dick Bowlin. "I drink too much pop, eat too much fast food. I have to stop eating all that if I'm gonna get in shape."

Bowlin didn't look happy. Perhaps they were on a shift when the fighting and shooting occurred. It looked like it had been a long night for them, but they gave off an aura of full-flavored professionalism. Competence. No-nonsense. Efficient. They were also polite. Both had addressed him as Mr. Mijares, but he told them to call him Mimi.

Blanco took out a pack of cigarettes. He plucked one out with his teeth and lit up. "Don't mind if I smoke, do you?"

Mimi shook his head.

"Can you tell us, in your own words, what happened?" asked Blanco.

"It wasn't our fault," Mimi said quickly. "We were having a few drinks. Luis asked this cute blonde girl if she wanted to dance. She said yes. They went out on the floor. That's when the rednecks approached."

"This is Arizona. We don't have rednecks here," Bowlin interjected. "If people think we have rednecks, it's bad for tourism. Let's just call them drunken white people."

"Well then, three drunken white people came up to us," Mimi said. "They started harassing Luis, telling him he didn't belong here and shouldn't be dancing with a white woman. They were not that polite. Ramon and I went over to protect our friend."

"So the six of you decided to take it outside?" asked Bowlin.

Mimi nodded. "After some insults and curses, we said we'll settle it outside. I didn't know that one of them was carrying a gun. You let people carry guns in bars here?"

"Law says they can. A lot of people like that law," replied Bowlin.

"Especially undertakers," Blanco added.

"So we went out and started fighting. I punched one guy twice then heard the gunshot. I turned around and Luis had fallen in the alley. His hands were over his stomach. I saw blood. He was groaning. The white guys just ran off. We called 911."

"Ever seen these guys before?" Bowlin asked.

"No."

"Well, the bartenders and others at the bar may know them," Blanco stated.

"We didn't do anything wrong. We were just having a drink and dancing. The rednecks started it."

The two detectives didn't respond. They both looked at him long and hard, as if they were studying his response. It made Mimi uncomfortable. Eventually, he broke the silence. "How's Luis?"

"The last we heard, your friend is in serious but stable condition. He's definitely alive but won't be playing baseball anytime soon," said Blanco.

A knock came to the door. The door opened and a uniformed officer poked his head in the room. "We have a lawyer here for Mr. Mijares."

Dang, that was quick.

Both Blanco and Bowlin got up and gathered their paperwork. "His client is free to go," said Blanco.

Mimi was escorted out of the interrogation room and back out to the lobby of the station where a short, balding lawyer in a sharp black suit waited. He approached Mimi and extended his hand. "Hello, Mimi, I'm Joe Amato. I was sent here by Marc Neufeld of the New York Yankees."

It was 3:00 a.m. when Mimi got home. He flopped onto his bed and fell asleep in his clothes. At 7:00 a.m. he was woken up by a call from Marc Neufeld, who was not happy. Marc did not want to hear Mimi explain his side of the story. Instead, he began scolding him. "Fair or not, you guys are a target. You have to be so careful about where you go and who you go with."

"I understand, but we weren't—"

"I'm flying you back to Tampa and we're going to have a talk about what it means to be a professional in our organization and how you must handle yourselves."

"What about the rest of the season?"

"Your Arizona experience is over."

After Marc hung up, Mimi looked around his Scottsdale apartment and began to shiver. Not from the cold, but from this hollow feeling in the pit of his stomach. He thought he might throw up. His face was sweating and his knees were weak, but he knew that he didn't have the flu. Reality was starting to sink in, and he realized how closely he had come to throwing away his dream to play for the Yankees, and baseball in general. He could have just as easily been the one to get shot. *From here on out, no more stupid mistakes.*

Mimi didn't want to leave the apartment. Rachel came over that night. They ordered food and watched a movie. He didn't want to talk about what happened, and she didn't push him. Rachel stayed the night, and they were both woken up the following morning at nine when there was a loud knock on the door. Mimi put on a shirt and left the bedroom to answer the door. He had no idea who was on the other side, but he certainly didn't expect to see Lola standing there with her arms out looking for a hug.

"I hope you like surprises. I just had to see you. I've missed you so much." As Lola stepped inside, Rachel came from the bedroom wearing nothing but one of Mimi's shirts. Nobody said a word. After a few long seconds of silence, Lola snapped. "How could you do this to me? You are so full of shit! I feel so stupid!"

It looked like she was about to cry, but that sadness quickly turned to rage. She started screaming obscenities as she swiped her arm across the nearby desk, knocking everything on the floor. Before Mimi could react, she stormed out and slammed the door behind her. Mimi felt shocked and numb. He looked at Rachel, who shrugged her shoulders. "Sorry," she said. "Come back to bed."

Mimi wanted to be alone and convinced Rachel to leave. He told her that he would call her later, but he had no intention of contacting her again. He knew his relationship with Lola had run its course and that she was not best person for him, but he still felt bad. Everything was falling apart.

The final blow came later that afternoon when he opened a package waiting for him at the stadium. It was from his mother in Cuba. Her letter, as usual, was heartwarming. She tried to cheer him up even though Mimi was well aware that she was living every day in fear and insecurity. The package included several photos of the family, including a few of Ozzie teaching a young Mimi to play baseball.

He didn't notice at first. It wasn't until he went back to look at the pictures a few hours later back at his apartment when one of the photos jumped out at him. It was a picture of Ozzie and one of his friends helping Mimi swing the bat. As Mimi continued to stare at the photograph, it became clear beyond a shadow of a doubt that Ozzie's friend was Willie's abuelo, Ivan.

"Oh my God! It's Ivan!"

Mimi let the photo fall to the ground. His mind raced. Suddenly it made so much sense. Ozzie knew Willie's father and grandfather. He thought back to Ozzie's words that day on the beach when they said goodbye before his first defection. Ozzie told Mimi to find Willie. To trust Willie. Ozzie would never say that lightly. Mimi suddenly felt sick. He felt like he betrayed his father and also betrayed Willie, who was a friend. He definitely missed their friendship and the long telephone conversations they would have about everything and anything. He wanted to speak to Willie about this whole Arizona experience. Why was he playing only one out of three games and why was he hitting only .200? Why was his mind wandering back to thoughts of Cuba? Why did his friend get shot? Why was he making stupid decisions about how to spend his time?

Mimi realized that leaving Willie was a mistake and one that he needed to make right.

Back to Florida

CHAPTER 23

It had been less than four weeks since Mimi left his apartment in Tampa, but when he walked back inside and turned on the lights, it felt like he had been gone a year. So much had changed.

He hadn't eaten in hours, but he also hadn't slept. He couldn't even think of unpacking so he left his bags by the door and went straight to the bedroom, where he flopped on the bed. He was seconds away from falling asleep when he noticed that he had a voicemail.

"Miguel Mijares, this is Assistant United States Attorney Charles Mann calling. I would like to speak to you about your dealings with and relationship with Guillermo 'Willie' Santos, who, as you probably know, has been charged with multiple felony counts of illegal smuggling. We can always subpoena you at some point, but I would rather just have you come to our office for a general chat. This does not necessarily mean that we will be calling you as a witness, but it is a possibility. Please me a call back at your earliest convenience."

Now Mimi was wide awake and he was scared. He immediately phoned Willie and told him what happened. They hadn't spoken in almost two months, but this was not the type of phone call either of them was expecting. Willie could tell that Mimi was nervous and told him to speak to a lawyer. Alex Harte was the only other lawyer Mimi knew, but he had no interest in contacting him about this matter.

"Let me call my lawyer, Rafael Velez, and see what he recommends," said Willie. "I don't think you should refuse to meet with Mann. If you do, he can just subpoena you down the road."

Willie arranged a time for Mimi to meet with Velez at his office. Mimi was back in Tampa only a few hours and he was experiencing another sleepless night. He found himself once again staring at the ceiling and wondering how he got himself into such a mess.

Mimi spent the next three days on edge. He had an appointment at 2:00 p.m. with Velez, and then Velez would accompany Mimi to the United States Attorney's office for a meeting with Mr. Mann.

Mimi was so nervous that he arrived a half hour early. The receptionist escorted him into Velez's office right away, and the tall lawyer stood to greet him with a warm smile. "Mr. Mimi Mijares, how are you doing? I heard you had a little setback in Arizona."

"Yes," said an embarrassed Mimi, who didn't want to talk about the fight.

"You're lucky to get out of that state alive in light of your skin color. They have their own ideas for how the law should apply to Hispanics."

"Actually, I found the two detectives, one of whom was Hispanic, to be professional. I thought they were good at their jobs."

"That's good to hear. Sometimes Arizona police will stop and arrest you just because of the way you look or speak. Immigration laws are supposed to be a matter in the exclusive jurisdiction of the federal government, but the State of Arizona is trying to lead the way for individual states to take control of immigration issues. But that's a story for another day. Please sit."

Velez sat down behind his desk and continued as Mimi pulled up his chair.

"I'm representing Willie in a federal criminal case charging him with illegally smuggling individuals, including yourself, from Cuba to the United States."

Velez seemed confident and that allowed Mimi to relax a little, even if he couldn't follow all of what he was saying.

"You are one of the Cuban defectors represented by Willie as an agent, at least you used to be represented by him. The prosecution is contacting some of these players to potentially help establish their case. The heart of their case relics primarily on the testimony of Jose Mesa and Felix Cardenas, who allegedly transported players after certain communications with Willie. In the interview later today, I expect Mr. Mann to ask you a series of questions concerning your relationship with Willie. Just answer truthfully and concisely. Do not volunteer information."

"Just like in Cuba," Mimi couldn't help but add. Even Velez smiled.

"The crucial point he will attempt to elicit is that Willie arranged for you to defect," added Velez.

"I never met or spoke to Willie until I was in the United States."

"Good," said Velez. "The more you minimize your knowledge and dealings with Willie before you arrived in the United States, the better it is for us. Mr. Mann may try to get you to say certain things that would prove that you knew or reasonably should have known that Willie was directly or indirectly responsible for your actual departure from Cuba. Do you understand what I am saying?"

"I get it."

"What about any of the people who helped you defect, both the first time and the second, did they ever mention the name Willie Santos?"

"No."

"So it's fair to say that, to the best of your knowledge, Willie Santos had no direct involvement in the planning of your defection?"

"Correct."

Mimi told Velez everything that he could remember. When he finished, they had a half hour before their meeting with Mann and spent the time talking about Cuba and family. Mimi was starting to feel comfortable around Velez and actually enjoyed their conversation.

At ten minutes before four, Velez grabbed his coat and walked with Mimi out of the office. They walked together down the street to the federal courthouse, which was an impressive architectural building. It reminded Mimi of some of the beautiful embassies in Havana.

Once they entered the building and stepped into the elevator, Mimi's anxieties returned and he felt a knot in the pit of his stomach. He had been in the United States now for about a year but still felt like an outsider, especially right now. Mimi came to this country to play baseball. He knew there would be challenges adjusting to American life, but he certainly never anticipated being in the middle of a legal dispute in a courtroom. This was not what he bargained for when he made the decision to defect.

Mimi and Velez exited the elevator on the twelfth floor. They walked down the hall and entered the United States Attorneys' office, which had a spacious reception area displaying a magnificent American flag along with numerous antique legal insignia. Velez approached the receptionist with a smile, "We are here for a meeting with Charles Mann."

She offered them water or soft drinks, but they both turned her down and waited in the lobby for a few minutes before Charles Mann entered to greet them. Mann made small talk with Velez as they made their way into Mann's large corner office. "How's it going, Raf? Staying busy?"

"Definitely. There's always something going on. You know that."

"Not that I want to tell you your business, Mr. Velez, but is it proper for you to represent a potential witness in this case while also representing the defendant? Could be a conflict of interest."

Velez gave a patronizing smile and said, "Of course, I have disclosed to Mr. Mijares and Mr. Santos all of the relevant factors surrounding my representation. As you well know, counselor, full disclosure is the key. Moreover, I have the right to interview potential witnesses as much as you do, so why don't we just proceed here and see where it goes."

Once they were all seated, Mann turned his attention to Mimi. "Welcome to the United States and congratulations on being a professional baseball player in the New York Yankees organization."

"Thank you."

"What I would very much like to hear is the story of how you defected."

"That's a little overly broad, don't you think, Mr. Mann," interjected Velez, just to be annoying. "Why don't you just ask him about his dealings with Willie Santos?"

"If it's all the same to you, I would prefer to ask my questions my own way when I am conducting an interview. But if I need your help, counselor, I will humbly ask it," said Mann, with a touch of aggravation in his voice. He looked down at his notes when his telephone rang. Mann answered the call, listened for a brief moment, then hung up. He quickly turned to Velez, and stated, "That's my secretary. She needs to see me for a couple of minutes. Excuse me, I'll be right back."

When Mann left the office, Velez reviewed his notes. Mimi stood to stretch his legs and checked out the various pictures on the wall, including one showing Mann shaking hands with President George W. Bush. Mimi's eyes scanned the walls. He admired the artwork and photographs. He particularly enjoyed the pictures of Mann fishing with his family, including one of him standing proudly next to a six-foot marlin. Then he noticed two beautifully framed diplomas from the University of Texas. Mimi's eyes gazed over the wall for a few more seconds but then abruptly returned to the diplomas. He walked right up to them standing inches away. One displayed Mann's degree from University of Texas undergraduate school in 1985 and the other from the University of Texas Law School . . . 1988. Then it hit him. Charles Mann was in the same undergraduate and law school class as Alex Harte. *Coincidence?*

Mr. Mann returned to his office. "I am very sorry about this, but I am going to have to re-schedule this interview. An emergency matter has come up and my appearance is needed before Judge Spiro right away. Raf, I will call you later this afternoon. My secretary will escort you out."

As they left the building, Velez whispered to Mimi, "That was strange. Maybe he thought you were going to come here without a lawyer. Once he saw me, he could have lost interest in conducting the interview."

"You think?"

"Emergencies come up, but he has enough associates in that office that any number of them could have spoken with Judge Spiro. He might have thought I would pick up clues on how he plans to prosecute Willie."

Velez received a call on his cell as Mimi's head continued to spin. After a few moments, Mimi spoke.

"I have no idea what this means but the agent who solicited me to fire Willie went to college and law school with Mann."

"How do you know?"

"I saw the diplomas on the wall."

"Just now?" asked an impressed Velez.

"Yeah, same university, same years. Undergraduate and law school. Strange, right? Do you think it means anything?"

"Maybe, maybe not. My job as your attorney is to see if I can take that information and use it to your advantage. There could be misconduct or there could be the perception of misconduct."

CHAPTER 24

Velez spent the next morning in court arguing motions in a drug conspiracy case. When he returned to his office, he immediately summoned Joanna to discuss the upcoming motion to dismiss that needed to be prepared for the Santos case.

"This is not one of those routine motions filed merely to protect the record on appeal. This could be the case right here, and I intend to let the judge know it. This must be a passionate, substantive motion. You need to research extensively, and I mean extensively, the Cuban Adjustment Act, the 'wet foot, dry foot' policy, and case law, which establishes our position that Willie reasonably believed that as soon as Mimi and the others touched dry land in the United States, their presence was lawful. The facts and the law will prove that regardless of whether or not Mimi had prior authorization to enter the United States, once he did arrive on our soil, he was lawfully entitled to seek political asylum and remain in the United States to play professional baseball. That is to say, Willie was unaware that the ballplayers did not have permission to come to the United States. In support of this position we will argue that the Cuban Adjustment Act and the 'wet foot, dry foot' policies of the U.S. Citizenship and Immigration Services make it reasonable for our client to have believed that the players could be brought here legally. These factors negate the necessary willful conduct, or mens rea, the prosecution needs to prove in order to convict Willie. The prosecution has to prove an unlawful intent which it cannot do since Willie clearly understood the players' presence in the United States to be lawful. Include in your research emotional examples of the repression Cuban citizens suffer at the hands of the Castro regime, etc., etc. I know there's a lot there, but time is crucial. Get me a memorandum by the end of the week. Oh, and include research of legislative and executive branch immigration regulative policies that apply specifically to Cubans."

For the next three days Joanna immersed herself in Section 8 United States Code #1255, otherwise known as the Cuban Adjustment Act. She was excited to undertake this research assignment, particularly because her parents were so obsessed with the Kennedys and she knew that JFK was somehow an important figure in establishing the history of our country's relationship with Cuba. When she was growing up, in her home there were dozens of books about John, Jackie, and the whole Kennedy clan. Joanna remembered studying the Bay of Pigs and the Cuban Missile Crisis while in high school. Her dad truly admired JFK, and her mom obsessed over Jackie. She recalled vividly the emotional conversations with her parents about the JFK assassination.

Joanna carefully researched court decisions that cited the Cuban Adjustment Act and also reviewed the many reports of the Immigration Naturalization Service dealing with policy toward Cuba. There were legislative hearings to digest and a series of laws passed by Congress, including the Trading with the Enemy Act and the Helms-Burton Law. There were countless articles and an exhaustive study of the numerous references on the internet. She engaged in a legal and historical exercise as she barely slept for the next three days. Then she walked into Mr. Velez office at about 8:00 p.m. carrying volumes of research and information.

"Okay, Jo, so what do we have?" Velez leaned back in his chair as Joanna handed him her memorandum, which sought to combine history with relevant case law, legislative hearing information, and directives from the Immigration Naturalization Service in order to make the case that these charges against Willie should be dismissed. She argued that the charges against Mr. Santos should be viewed in the context of fifty years' worth of United States policies with Cuba and that, as a matter of law, Willie did not have the necessary criminal intent, "mens rea," or scienter to commit the crimes charged. She effectively pointed out that while the government here charged Willie with profiteering, there was actually no evidence or even allegation of commercial gain to Willie's benefit.

"I hope you approve, Mr. Velez. I feel pretty good about the merits of our argument. One thing I would like to add if possible is an affidavit executed by Mimi Mijares, confirming that he came to the United States for a lawful purpose, to play baseball, has no criminal record, and that the defendant Guillermo Santos promptly arranged for him to meet with an immigration attorney to appropriately, legally process his application for asylum and parole. That document would definitely bolster the arguments made in the brief."

"Good idea. I'll work on that," said Velez as he grabbed his coat.

His mind was already on the next step. As he rushed out of the office for his next meeting, he pulled out his phone and dialed the number for private investigator Denny Biler. Over the past couple years Velez had turned to Biler frequently because he found him thorough and reliable. He always had a difficult time making small talk with Biler, but that didn't matter because his firm did good work.

"Denny! I'm representing a client in a federal criminal matter that I might need your help on."

"For you? Always," joked Biler. "What's up?"

"How would you like to look into the business dealings of a U.S. attorney and a sports agent?"

CHAPTER 25

The next day, Velez, Joanna, and Willie stood before the judge in court as he told them, "I have read defendant's motion to dismiss as well as the government's motion in opposition together with the supporting memoranda. I am ready to hear oral arguments. Mr. Velez, it's your motion."

As Velez began to rise from his chair, Assistant United States Attorney Mann abruptly stood up and proclaimed to the court, "If I may, Your Honor, the government moves to strike the affidavit of Miguel Mijares attached as Exhibit A to defendant's motion and to disregard any arguments made that directly or indirectly rely on said affidavit. We have no opportunity to cross-examine the witness as to matters contained in the affidavit and therefore this testimony should be stricken for purposes of this motion. Mr. Mijares will have every opportunity to testify at trial where both parties will be able to question him. It would violate the due process requirement of the constitution for this court to accept the facts stated in the affidavit without our right to cross-examine."

"Would you like to respond to that, Mr. Velez?" inquired Judge Shields.

"Yes, indeed. I find counsel's point very curious, particularly since Mr. Mann has interviewed Mr. Mijares and is fully aware of the facts stated in the affidavit. There are no surprises here. Moreover, certainly the government has had ample time to put forth its own evidence that might contradict facts stated in the affidavit at issue, if any such evidence were to exist."

After furrowing his eyebrows in disdain, Judge Shields stated, "I am inclined to grant the government's request to strike the affidavit. A party's opportunity to cross-examine witnesses concerning material facts is an important element of due process."

As the judge paused, Velez rose and offered the following: "Let me make a suggestion. Allow us to proceed with our oral arguments as scheduled. If the court feels at the end of the arguments that it is necessary to produce Mr. Mijares as a live witness, it shall be incumbent upon us to produce him. Otherwise, the portion of the arguments relating to the affidavit shall be stricken. That way Mr. Mann will have the opportunity to cross-examine and confront Mr. Mijares if he so desires and if this court deems it necessary. We suggest the court defer its ruling on this issue until the arguments are presented. It's not like we are in front of a jury at this time that would be prejudiced."

"Fair enough," the judge stated before Mann had a chance to reply. "Although I will tell you right now that I am leaning heavily toward requiring the affiant's live testimony subject to cross-examination by the government attorneys."

Rafael Velez had anticipated this entire exchange. Mimi had been extensively prepared by Velez and Joanna for the possibility of live testimony. He was a telephone call away. Truth be told, Velez actually wanted Mimi Mijares to testify in open court as part of this hearing on the motion to dismiss.

"May I proceed, Your Honor?" inquired Velez.

"By all means."

Velez walked slowly to the center of the courtroom. He paused for effect and cast a glare toward the attorneys at the government's table. He was normally a jovial man who enjoys exchanging pleasantries even with his adversaries, now it was game on.

"Let me begin, Your Honor, by pointing out that my client, Guillermo 'Willie' Santos, is the first person in this country's glorious history to be criminally charged with smuggling a baseball player into the country. We have had at least fifty baseball players defect here from Cuba over many years. And, of course, thousands of non-baseball playing Cubans have defected to America. Fortunately we have a United States court system that can even tell its own government that it has gone too far, that it has exceeded its discretion and I intend to clearly make the case substantively and legally that this criminal prosecution, as a matter of law, must be dismissed. This is massive waste of taxpayers' dollars and I will focus on the specific facts and law before this court."

"That would be appreciated," interjected Mann, rising to object.

Velez threw Mann a stare intended to rattle as he walked around the courtroom like a matador. Velez was cooking now, clearly in his element.

"I do not believe even for a second that our Congress intended for the United States Code, in particular 8 USC #1324, to have a result where an American citizen can be prosecuted even though he acted consistently with INS requirements, congressional action, and frankly, fifty years of American history. Section 1324, which forms the basis of the criminal indictment here, states, and I quote, 'Any person who, knowing an alien has not received prior official authorization to come to, enter or reside in the United States, brings to the United States such alien in furtherance of such violation for the purpose of obtaining commercial advantage or private financial gain shall be subject to various penalties.'" Velez removed his glasses as he continued. "An essential element, therefore, is that the defendant acted in furtherance of the alien's intent to remain in the United States illegally . . . for commercial advantage. The cases are cited in our brief, which makes it clear that such proof is required to establish that the defendant acted willfully and with the necessary specific intent, or mens rea, to commit a crime. The Court decision from the 7th Circuit Court of Appeals specifically stated that any violation of 1324(a)(1)(B) must include proof that the defendant acted *willfully.* And the case cited from the 11th Circuit makes it clear that the element of commercial advantage/private financial gain is critical.

A review of the legislative history, case law, and INS policies in connection with the charging statute reveals that the prosecution here abused its discretion and exceeded its authority in deciding to prosecute. The Cuban immigrants in question, for example, Mr. Mijares, came here to seek political asylum and stay for a lawful purpose. Our position is supported by the Cuban Adjustment Act—8 USC 1255 enacted in 1966. Moreover, the so-called wet-foot, dry foot policy consistently has been enforced by this country and is referred to in the Meissner memo, which became the policy of the INS. These provisions and case law precedent are cited in our brief. The stated purpose, according to the testimony before Congress, of the Cuban Adjustment Act, explicitly provides that the status of a Cuban native who has been inspected or paroled into the United States, which was accomplished in the Mr. Mijares' case, thanks to the actions of my client along with the assistance of an immigration attorney, may be adjusted by the Attorney General allowing the individual to be lawfully admitted for permanent residence. Your Honor, the application and legislative history of the Cuban Adjustment Act would deem it obvious that Mijares and the other ballplayers would so qualify, and my client, Guillermo Santos, acted accordingly. More examples of the legislative history, the purpose of the Act, and additional case law are described in our brief. It is interesting to note that the legislative history consistently speak to the political and economic repression that Cuban citizens endure at the hands of Fidel Castro. Our country even endorsed a series of freedom flights between 1965 and 1971 to help these Cubans in certain situations. And now we are here criminally prosecuting a person who took all the proper steps to help such an individual?" This question by Velez was proffered with a combination of sarcasm and disdain.

Velez walked slowly to his counsel table and began to take a drink of water before continuing when Mann rose to object. "Your Honor, this history lesson may be interesting to some but has nothing to do with the case at hand."

The judge responded, "You may have a point, but I'll give a little latitude."

Velez continued undeterred. "The case law cited makes it clear that in the absence of a disqualifying criminal record or other similar factors that would bar CAA adjustment, there was no criminal intent or willful conduct to justify criminal prosecution. This notion is further confirmed in the so-called Meissner Memorandum, a copy of which is attached to our motion, in which the head of the Department of Immigration Naturalization Service reiterated the American policy that a Cuban refugee who reaches U.S. land be allowed to stay, apply for political asylum and residency. Doris Meissner was commissioner of the INS from 1993 to 2000, and she issued a memorandum to all regional directors entitled 'Eligibility for Permanent Residence Under the Cuban Adjustment Act Despite Having Arrived At A Place Other Than A Designated Port of Entry.' In it she directed the INS to incorporate a policy to generously construe the CAA citing in the Matter of Mesa, also detailed in our brief. The memorandum also references 'urgent humanitarian reasons' that necessitated this type of conduct toward Cuban defectors. For all these reasons, it would be unconscionable to continue this criminal prosecution against Mr. Santos particularly since he immediately began the necessary steps to take Mr. Mijares legally through the immigration process. As indicated in the affidavit of Mr. Mijares, plus the other INS documents attached to our motion, the defendant here immediately arranged for and participated in a meeting with immigration attorney Hillman in order to comply with our country's laws and policies. Is that the conduct of a person engaged in criminal activity? Let's get real here. The very purpose of that meeting was to take the appropriate steps, consistent with our immigration laws. As a direct result of my client's conduct, Mr. Mijares was processed by the INS, responded accordingly in a timely manner to every request that was put to him. The Cuban baseball players in question came to the United States for a lawful purpose, so they could be granted asylum and paroled in accordance with the federal immigration policy governing the status of Cuban refugees, as expressed in the Cuban Adjustment Act, the Meissner Memorandum, and the wet foot-dry foot policy. Mr. Santos had the reasonable belief that when Mr. Mijares entered the United States and he provided the proper paperwork for him to be here legally and seek asylum, that such conduct negates specific criminal intent." Velez shrugged and took a deep breath before proceeding.

"Moreover, the government is in possession of bank statements and financial disclosures of the defendant. As part of our motion to dismiss, we have attached as an exhibit a summary of those documents. The parties have stipulated to the accuracy of the financial summary which goes back several years into the business of defendant Santos."

As the judge paged through the motion until he found the financial summary document, Velez continued, "It is clear from the exhibit that Mr. Santos not only did not obtain commercial or financial gain from the conduct alleged in the indictment, he actually lost money. A material element of the indictment states, and I quote, the defendant's purpose was to obtain commercial advantage or financial gain in violation of 8 USC 1324 and 18 USC," Velez paused. "That just did not happen here and the government has so stipulated. That's because the truth is that

Guillermo Santos did not act with the primary purpose of personal financial gain but rather for the purpose of assisting people in need." Another pause as Velez walked toward his counsel table. "Now it's up to this honorable court to do the just thing and dismiss these charges. Thank you, Your Honor."

"Thank you, Mr. Velez," said Judge Shields. "Mr. Mann, your response."

Assistant United States Attorney Mann took a final look at his notes and rose with a legal pad in hand to address the court. "Whether Mr. Santos had the requisite intent to commit a crime is a matter for the jury to decide, not this court. It is a question of fact, not of law. Mr. Velez is attempting to distract this court. The fact that Cubans may be eligible to seek adjustment of their status under applicable immigration laws does not make it legal to smuggle Cuban aliens into this country prior to that adjustment of status. This case is not about conditions in Cuba. It is not about Fidel Castro. It is not about baseball. It is about whether this defendant conspired to bring individuals to the United States, for his own commercial advantage, by the way, without having legal permission to do so. Just because Mr. Mijares may have been eligible for an adjustment of his immigration status once he arrived here does not excuse Santos from the smuggling and transporting. Neither the INA nor the CAA authorizes uninspected Cuban aliens to wander the United States without the knowledge of or inspection by immigration officials. Mijares was unlawfully present until such time as he was presented for inspection and paroled. Your Honor, this is why the term 'adjustment' is used in the Cuban Adjustment Act. The status of an alien such as Mr.

Mijares was not lawful until it was adjusted." Mann then asked the judge to deny defendant's motion to dismiss, thanked the court, and returned to his seat.

Judge Shields looked down as he paged through some of the notes he was taking during oral arguments. After a few minutes he looked up and stated that he would like to hear the live testimony of Miguel Mijares as part of the hearing on the motion to dismiss. "How quickly can you produce him?" the judge asked Mr. Velez.

After huddling with Joanna for a moment, Velez responded, "We can have him in this courtroom tomorrow morning."

"Very well then. This matter will be continued at 9:00 a.m. tomorrow." The judge then banged his gavel, left the bench abruptly, and the court was adjourned.

The attorneys looked at each other. No one could tell which way the court was leaning based on the judge's reactions and questions. Velez did indicate to Willie and Joanna that, on balance, he was encouraged by the fact that the judge wanted Mimi in court to testify. "He could have just denied the motion to dismiss if he was so inclined and left Mimi to testify at trial in front of the jury. It makes sense that for the judge to consider a dismissal at this juncture of the case, he would want to hear the live testimony of Mimi subject to my direct examination as well as the government's cross-examination. The judge then is in a position to assess the credibility of the witness. The good news is that this judge will not be afraid to do what he believes is right and he has the power to do whatever he wants."

CHAPTER 26

The anxiety in Mimi's stomach as he approached the witness stand was profound. He had never testified in a courtroom before anywhere.

Mimi felt prepared. He had spent a great deal of time going over the process with Velez and even more so with Joanna, who previewed all the possible questions and told him he had nothing to worry about. "Just tell the truth," is what she told him. She advised him to answer only the specific questions asked and to give his best recollection of events. Velez often reminded him that it was okay to say that he didn't recall an event if that was the case. "It's natural to not remember details that may have occurred months or even years ago," Velez told him.

The bailiff swore in Mimi and Mr. Velez began with some easy background questions. He then asked Mimi to tell the story of his defection.

Charles Mann took extensive notes and gathered his thoughts for cross-examination. He listened to Mimi admit that he drove with Jose Mesa and Felix Cardenas to see Willie once he arrived in the United States. It seems a reasonable assumption that there had to have been communication before Mimi even departed Cuba. Mann had the statements of Felix and Jose, who would testify that Mimi identified Willie as his agent while still in Cuba prior to the first attempt to defect.

"Are you represented by an agent?" asked Mr. Velez.

"Yes. Right now my agent is Alexander Harte. Previously, my agent was Willie Santos, but I changed this past October."

As Mimi stated the name of Alexander Harte, he looked right at the prosecuting attorney as Mr. Velez told him to do. Velez followed with a glare of his own toward Mann as he carefully maneuvered his way around the courtroom. Suddenly Mann looked very uneasy. In fact, he rubbed his stomach as if it was hurting. His face turned pale and it looked like he might throw up. Mann could no longer focus on Mimi's testimony. His mind wandered back to a time when he was working on the CSEMMG antitrust case. Yes, he communicated with Harte but certainly did nothing illegal. Velez considered it a minor victory to see Mann appear off guard as he continued to question Mimi about his dealings with defendant Willie Santos, his experience with the immigration attorney Paul Hillman, as well as his experiences with immigration officials. Mimi clearly stated that he had no contact with Willie while he was in Cuba directly or indirectly. He only heard of Willie by reputation. He did eventually hire Willie to be his agent and vaguely agreed to pay him a fee to be determined although he had not paid him anything yet.

"It became clear to me that Willie was not doing this for the money, but for his passion to help the oppressed people in Cuba," said Mimi.

Velez continued to ask Mimi to elaborate on the matters contained in his affidavit. He was now relaxed and gaining confidence as a witness. As for Mr. Mann, he didn't appear nearly as confident. When Mr. Velez concluded his questioning of Mimi, the judge asked Mann if he would like to cross-examine the witness.

Mann sat quietly for a moment before shockingly and weakly saying, "No, thank you. No questions." His mind was flashing back to a couple of meetings for drinks he had with Alexander Harte. Harte pumped him for information about the CSEMMG matter before the antitrust division of the United States' Attorney's office and maybe he was too happy to oblige. But Harte never mentioned that he was trying to steal Mimi Mijares as a client from Willie Santos. Santos was small potatoes.

Mann's associate, an older prosecutor, looked at him in disbelief. He knew how long they had prepared for this court case and cross-examination. This made absolutely no sense to him.

"This hearing on defendant's motion to dismiss is hereby concluded," Judge Shields stated. "It is my intention to issue a ruling within three days. I will do so electronically, no need to appear in open court. We are adjourned."

Velez smiled as Mann and his associate quickly gathered their papers and left the courtroom without a word.

On the way out of the courtroom, Velez spoke to Willie and Mimi. He tried to downplay expectations, pointing out the very low percentage of times in which a defendant can get an indictment dismissed as a result of a pretrial motion. "It's usually a lot easier and safer for a judge to just let the case go to trial rather than effectively taking the case out of the hands of the prosecution and the jury." Velez did say that he liked this particular motion to dismiss based on the facts, the law, and the intangible emotional pull in Willie's favor. "Now we wait three days and see what happens. Willie, I want you to come to my office Friday morning. That's the day we should have a decision on our motion. No matter how it turns out, there are matters we need to discuss."

"No problem, I'll be there," Willie responded. Once they were outside, Mimi embraced Willie and wrapped him in a big hug. They didn't have to speak. Each knew how the other felt. Willie was grateful to Mimi for taking the time and effort to testify on his behalf. Mimi was grateful to Willie for so many things, especially remaining his friend despite his stupid actions that led to leaving him as his agent.

CHAPTER 27

Velez walked into his office promptly at 8:30 Friday morning to find that the electronic decision from Judge Shields had just been received. Velez printed it out, sat at his desk, held the opinion tightly, and read:

"This court has received and reviewed defendant's motion to dismiss together with the government's written response. The parties have both filed extensive briefs in support of their respective positions. An evidentiary hearing and oral argument was held in open court with attorneys and parties present. It is this court's order as fully explained in the attached memorandum opinion that defendant's motion to dismiss is hereby granted as to all charges and the indictment against him is dismissed. The government has seven days to appeal this order."

Velez nearly exploded out of his chair. Not normally one to show too much emotion, this time he could not contain himself. He started to call Willie, but decided to wait until he came to the office to tell him in person.

Velez walked into Joanna's small office and slapped his hands together, causing her to almost jump from her chair. "We won.

The judge granted the motion to dismiss. I've e-mailed the opinion to you."

Joanna smiled brightly with delight.

Velez returned to his office to read and soak in the entire opinion. Judge Shields began with a legal discussion of criminal intent, scienter, and mens rea as a requirement of the #1324 offense charged in the indictment, but spent most of the twenty page opinion reviewing United States immigration policy as it pertains to the status of Cuban defectors. The court basically concluded that even if defendant Santos arranged to bring Mijares to the United States (for which the government alleged but currently had no such direct evidence), he did so for a lawful purpose so that Mijares could be granted asylum and paroled in accordance with federal immigration policy. The opinion heavily relied on the cases cited by Velez along with the application and intent of the Cuban Adjustment Act and the wet foot, dry foot policy followed by this country. The court also referred to the Immigration Nationality Act as proof that under these circumstances the government would not be able to satisfy the mens rea requirement as a matter of law in part because it was uncontradicted that Mr. Santos did not primarily act for the purpose of personal financial gain. Basically, it was this judge's opinion that the prosecution exceeded its discretion in pursuing this case.

Velez could not remember enjoying reading a legal decision as much as this one. He was really looking forward to communicating the news to Willie. As he smiled, he thought to himself how sometimes lawyers have good news to relay to clients and sometimes they have bad news. It is certainly a lot more fun to give a client good news, and Velez intended to relish the moment.

When Willie arrived at Velez's office a short while later, Velez thought about dragging out the story and maybe playing coy, but decided this was too important to play any games. He got right to it. "We received very good news today. Our motion was granted and all charges against you are dismissed for the time being. The government has seven days to file a notice of appeal to the First Circuit Court of Appeals. But for right now, it's all good. We could not have asked for a better, stronger opinion from the court."

Willie felt blood rush from his toes up to his brain after hearing the news. He hesitated only a moment before he jumped into the attorney's arms while looking to the heavens. "Mr. Velez, thank you so much. I don't know what to say. You are the greatest lawyer ever!"

Willie hugged Velez and then hugged Joanna when she walked into the office. "Excuse me while I call my wife," exclaimed Willie, as he went into the small conference room to privately share the good news with the person who had been suffering the most during this process. As soon as she picked up, he shouted, "Honey, we won! Our motion was granted, and the charges against me have been dismissed."

Marilyn screamed and cried tears of joy. "Thank you, God, thank you. Is this all over now?"

"Not entirely. They do have the right to appeal this ruling, but today is a very good day."

Once Willie was back in Velez's office, the attorney explained how the appeal process worked and stated, "I have a possible game plan that may dissuade Mr. Mann from appealing."

Willie wasn't sure exactly what that meant, but by that time all he wanted to do was go home and relax with his wife.

CHAPTER 28

Manny and Anna Mijares were escorted to a private jet at Havana Airport by one of Fidel's right-hand men by the name of Pedro Azul. Along with a small group of Cuban businessmen and dignitaries, they boarded the plane bound for Miami.

Manny was nervous. For some reason he was waiting for the police to board the plane and pull him and his mother off so he held his breath until the plane left the ground. Once in the air, he stared down at the island of Cuba as the plane gained altitude. Unlike Mimi, Manny had resigned himself to the fact that he would live and die on this island run by despots and psychopaths. He did not know whether to laugh or cry because he hadn't yet wrapped his head around what was going on. It was only twenty-four hours earlier that they were notified that they would receive visas to visit Mimi in Miami.

Manny and Anna spoke only to each other during the flight. They didn't know anybody else on board. Upon arriving at Miami International Airport, they were met by Father Garcia, Marc Neufeld's assistant Luis Montanez, immigration attorney Paul Hillman, and Willie's assistant Claudia, who warmly embraced them. The group entered a van and proceeded to Willie's office where they arrived at 5:00 p.m.

Manny and Anna were both confused and excited as they entered the building. Anna was especially confused. It almost felt like she was having an out-of-body experience. Claudia took her aside to explain what was going on and assured here that everything would be fine. "You are going to see Mimi in a matter of minutes," said Claudia.

Once inside his office, Willie greeted Anna and Manny with a big smile. "I am so happy to meet you both." He hugged Manny first, and then Anna. "Mimi is on his way here. He might have a heart attack when he sees you. Actually, it's going to lift his spirits so much. He is aware that we've been working to make this happen, but he has no idea that today is the day. Come in here to the conference room, relax and sit down on the couch. I will get you some water."

A half hour later, Mimi pulled into the garage of Willie's building for what he thought was going to be a meeting about him returning as a client. Mimi had been at Yankee's spring training for a week now and had made up his mind to drop Harte and return to Willie, but they hadn't officially signed the papers yet. When he stepped off the elevator and entered the reception area, he saw that Claudia had a strange look on her face. She could barely control her emotions and the smile on her face just kept getting bigger. "Are you okay?" asked Mimi.

"Sure, absolutely. I'll go tell Willie you're here."

Willie came to greet Mimi in the reception area. Mimi immediately wrapped him in a hug and said, "I never told you how sorry I am that I left you for Harte. It's the stupidest thing I've ever done in my life, by far. Please forgive me and will you please be my agent again?"

The two laughed.

"Of course. Don't worry about it, Mimi. We all make mistakes as we go through various phases and experiences in our lives. It's part of maturing and growing up. Once this whole legal situation is cleared up, I would love to represent you. Here, let's go in the conference room."

Mimi followed Willie in the conference room and his jaw dropped at the sight of his mom. His heart skipped a beat and he needed to do a double take because he thought he was dreaming. He could not believe what he was seeing. It had been just over a year, but it seemed like a lifetime since he laid eyes on his mother. He realized this was not a dream. Right in front of him was his mother and brother. Mimi did not even try to fight back tears.

Anna couldn't believe it either, but was slowly and surely realizing that she was being reunited with her oldest son. A surreal look of happiness combined with more than a touch of bewilderment overcame her as she hugged Mimi for several minutes. Both of them cried uncontrollably. Mimi then went over to embrace Manny. Nothing was said; nothing needed to be said. No words could have encapsulated what any of them were feeling at that moment. For Mimi, it felt as if he had been living in darkness and suddenly there was light.

The reunion proved to be bittersweet for Anna when, a half hour later, she joined Mimi, Manny, Claudia, and Willie in his office to hear a serious presentation from Mr. Pedro Azul. The tiny man in a suit explained the legalities of their visit. "I am serving as Anna and Manny's host while in the United States. Mr. Guillermo Santos, with major assistance from the New York Yankees as well as Father Garcia and Cardinal Mercado, were able to obtain a fifteen-day visa for Anna and Manny to accompany this important group of Cuban businessmen and officials visiting the United States. As you may be aware, currently United States citizens are able to visit Cuba as part of an arts or educational program. Let me say right up front, however, it would be a big mistake to refuse to follow all of the rules and, of course, for you to try to defect. There would definitely be repercussions on a lot of levels. I have spoken to Mr. Santos, who is responsible for you, as well as Mr. Hillman. As you know, you are each wearing a tracking device for us to monitor your whereabouts 24/7. I will return to this office in five days to meet with Anna and Manny, again in ten days, and finally in fifteen days, at which time you must be prepared to depart the United States and return to Cuba. Mr. Santos has my telephone number if you wish to reach me. Of course I have your telephone numbers here and will be checking in regularly. Any questions before I leave?"

Azul received no response. Anna began to cry. Mimi and Manny embraced her, trying to provide comfort. She certainly was happy to see Mimi, but looked and felt like a fish out of water. She was a stranger in a strange land.

Slowly, the three of them left the office arm in arm. By the time they reached Mimi's car, they all started to loosen up. Mimi assured both his mother and brother, "I have plenty of room in my apartment. You guys are going to love it here. I am so happy to see the both of you."

"So tell me about the New York Yankees," Manny said, changing the subject. "How has major league camp been going?"

"Manny, it's unbelievable. I showed up for my first day of major league spring training with the New York fucking Yankees one week ago. And there they were: Derek Jeter, Jorge Posada, and my two all-time favorite players, Robinson Cano and Mariano Rivera. Mo actually came up and spoke to me. What a nice man. Total class. I think I was more excited that day than for any baseball game I ever played in my entire life. I was in center field taking outfield practice, firing throws to Jeter and Cano. It was amazing. The day after tomorrow is our first spring training game and you guys are coming. Willie is going to pick you up and bring you to the game."

Manny hung on Mimi's every word as he talked about major league spring training and the New York Yankees. Anna, on the other hand, seemed to care less. As thrilled as she was to see Mimi, she could not shake that dazed and confused feeling.

Mimi put his arm around her. "Mom, this may seem overwhelming right now. But it's fine. Relax."

Anna hugged her son. With tears in her eyes, she said, "I was thinking I would never see you again and now I am in the United States."

"Let's say we go out for a little shopping," Mimi suggested.

Supermarkets are routine in America. They are convenient, usually very clean and organized. Customers often get to know the checkout ladies and gentlemen. But for someone from a third-world country, what is routine to Americans can seem as breathtaking as the Grand Canyon.

When they walked into a rather large Publix store, Anna was cautious, walking like a woman negotiating through broken glass, with Mimi and Manny at her side. But her breath almost left her when she looked at the meat section. There was a long line of packaged meats that looked to her as long as a football field. In neatly wrapped cellophane, the packages sparkled under the store's lights. First was the ground beef. Beyond that were pork chops, six and eight to a carton, lined up six rows deep. Chicken too. Chicken was everywhere. Thighs, legs, wings, breasts. Anna shook her head. For a moment she felt faint as her legs almost weakened.

"Momma, are you all right?" Mimi asked as he grabbed her arm and steadied her.

"Do you remember how we could barely find food to eat?"

"Yes. There were shortages of everything. Many families faced what we did."

Anna nodded. She spread out her hands. "Look at this. All this food. All this abundance. We never saw anything like this in Cuba. There can't be any hunger here. I've never seen anything like this."

Wait until she sees Wal-Mart, Mimi thought. Food, clothing, jewelry, books, drugs, guns, and everything in between.

Anna slowly leaned over and picked up a carton of ground beef. Most customers simply flopped the meat into their shopping cart, but Anna gently lowered the package until it touched the metal. She paused for a moment before lifting another package of meat. Mimi smiled. If his mother was this impressed by the meat department, she was going to be wowed by the veggie section.

CHAPTER 29

"No interruptions. Hold my calls," Rafael Velez advised his secretary, as he closed the door to his office, which was something he rarely did. His game face returned but with a slight smirk as he dialed the direct line of Charlie Mann.

"Hi, Charlie, this is Rafael Velez."

Mann chuckled once under his breath. "So what is this, you called to gloat about your victory in the Santos case?"

"Yes, I guess you could say that, although no one would accuse me of being the type to gloat. You may disagree, but I thought Judge Shields nailed it in his well-thought-out and thorough opinion. The Appellate Court will have a difficult time reversing such a well-reasoned decision. Actually, the main purpose of this call is to make a few points as you consider whether to even bother to appeal the ruling."

Velez paused to let that sink in. "Not sure where to begin, Charlie, but interesting questions arose during our investigation as we prepared for our defense of this case. We have been working with the private eye Denny Biler, and issues came to light that the Attorney Disciplinary Committee might like to review as well as the Major League Baseball Players Association concerning your law license and the agent certification of Alexander Harte, your classmate at the University of Texas."

Velez waited for a response and when none came from Mann, he continued, "This is what we learned: Number one, both you and Harte went to undergraduate college and law school at the University of Texas where you were classmates. Number two, you and Mr. Harte were teammates on that college baseball team. Number three, a few years ago as an Assistant United States Attorney you worked closely with the Federal Communication Commission and the Justice Department concerning a criminal and civil investigation regarding possible antitrust violations, the circumventing of laws by operating shell companies, and other shady practices by a company known as Creative Sports Entertainment Media Management Group, CSEMMG. Eventually you helped finalize a consent decree settlement quite favorable to CSEMMG. Shortly thereafter CSEMMG apparently offered to purchase the agency owned by Alexander Harte for $35 million. Somewhere along the line, Harte stole Mimi Mijares as a client. On and on, there's more, but you get the idea. I don't claim to know everything or even know what all of this means, but something here doesn't pass the smell test. I have no idea at this point whether you had been communicating with your old college teammate, whether this may have influenced the investigation into CSEMMG or, worst of all, whether you stood to benefit from this series of transactions. All that said, let me put it this way, Mr. Mann, right now I have concluded that there is not enough substantive information to forward a complaint to the Attorney

Disciplinary Committee. Moreover, even though Biler is eager to keep investigating, I don't feel like paying him anymore. Frankly, I would rather not continue this investigation. But if you decide to appeal Judge Shields' ruling I may have no choice but to further educate myself as to your history and relationship with Alex Harte as well as your handling of the CSEMMG matter. Depending on the factors that emerge, the Attorney Disciplinary Committee and the MLBPA may have to be notified."

Talk about hard ball. Mann wanted to scream but thought better of it. He forced himself to keep his cool before he responded.

"Listen, Raf, there is nothing there. You are stretching to reach conclusions that are not factually based for leverage in this case. I have rarely spoken to Alex Harte over the last several years. And I certainly did not know that he stole Mr. Mijares as a client. My decision as to whether or not to appeal Judge Shields' order will be based on the merits of the appeal. Nothing else."

After the two attorneys said goodbye and hung up their phones, Mann stared at the ceiling, motionless for a moment. He slowly walked over to a file cabinet in the corner of his office and removed two things: a bottle of Maker's Mark and an e-mail exchange between him and Alex Harte. The Maker's Mark was generally reserved for celebrating court victories, but not today. Mann walked over to a small refrigerator, put a handful of ice cubes in a glass, filled it with the whiskey, and took a big gulp. He reflected on his role in the CSEMMG investigation several years prior as he reviewed an e-mail from Alex Harte, which read in part: "Good job resolving the CSEMMG matter with the Justice Department. Thanks for your efforts in leading to that settlement.

FYI, the $35 million stock purchase agreement between my agency and CSEMMG is scheduled for closing next month. Let's stay in touch. I will look forward to our next lunch date."

Mann thought about the handful of meetings, telephone conversations, and emails with Harte about the CSMEEG matter that took place before, during, and after the investigation into that company's possible improprieties. He took another gulp of Maker's.

***

Later that afternoon, Willie was running a little late as he hustled to get to his daughter's soccer game. The game had already started as he joined Marilyn on the sidelines. They cheered mightily as Katie nearly scored a goal, only to be stopped by an excellent play by the goalie. When Willie grabbed his cell phone to view a text he had just received, Marilyn gave him one of those annoying looks. She hated that he checked his cell phone when he should be enjoying his family, but when he showed her this text, all was forgiven. It was from Rafael Velez and it read: "I am very pleased to advise that seven days have now passed without the government appealing the order dismissing charges against you. You are a free man."

Willie gave Marilyn a long kiss right there in the stands.

CHAPTER 30

The next day, Willie picked up Anna and Manny so they could attend the first spring training game of the year. It was the New York Yankees versus Baltimore Orioles. Manny was quite familiar with the Baltimore Orioles and remembered when they came to Cuba to play an exhibition game in March of 1999.

In the car going to the game, Willie quietly told them, "Despite what Mr. Azul said, there could definitely be a path for you guys to defect. I've already looked into it and spoken to our immigration attorney, as well as other respected members in the Cuban-American community. There are plenty of us willing to help."

Willie kept talking, but Anna tuned out. Neither she nor Manny responded to the notion of defecting. In fact, they were not very comfortable with the conversation. Willie was gung-ho that every possible Cuban should want to leave for a better life in America, but it was not that easy for Anna and Manny, especially after they had just been read the riot act by Mr. Azul. They were able to obtain fifteen-day visitation visas with strict conditions attached, and when the officials indicate there could be repercussions, Manny and Anna believed they meant it. That said, they still politely digested what Willie had to say.

Willie parked the car in the stadium parking lot and the three began walking toward the field. Manny's heart began to race when he saw the sign, "Tampa Stadium—Spring Training Home of the New York Yankees." *Here, baseball stadiums are beautiful. Artistic, symmetrical, green, and perfect,* he thought.

They arrived early enough to watch infield/outfield practice. In many ways this was Manny's favorite part of baseball. Now he was mesmerized. The timing and flow of a coach hitting ground balls to the infielders and outfielders was an art form. The routine was the same, whether it was happening in the U.S.A., Cuba, Dominican Republic, Venezuela, Japan, or anywhere else organized baseball was played. Manny focused on the infielders as they gracefully moved around, covered their bases, and whipped the ball around. Mimi was currently one of three positioned in centerfield. Manny couldn't take his eyes off his big brother. Even Anna was starting to smile as she saw how excited Manny was watching the pre-game workouts.

Out in the field, Mimi charged a line drive that was hit to center. He caught it after the first hop and fired a bullet to second base. Another ball was hit to Mimi that he caught in the air and fired to third base, followed by another, which he threw right on target to home plate. Manny had seen Mimi do this thousands of times over the years, but never enjoyed it more than he did today. Each throw was perfect. Even Jeter gave Mimi an approving smile.

Following infield/outfield practice Mimi ran off the field with a big smile on his face as he observed Manny on the other side of the fence. As he approached Manny, several fans stopped him for his autograph. He was more than happy to oblige and to engage in conversation. Mimi signaled for Manny to come with him and together they went into the Yankee clubhouse.

Manny thought he died and went to heaven as Mimi introduced him to Robinson Cano, Mariano Rivera, and Derek Jeter. Manny couldn't believe this was happening. Players were joking around in the clubhouse. Mimi was as happy and outgoing as Manny had ever seen him.

The time came for Mimi to walk Manny back to his seat next to Anna and Willie in the stands. Mimi made sure to shake Willie's hand again. "Thank you for everything, Willie."

"That's what friends are for." Tears of joy came to Mimi's eyes as he returned to the field to rejoin his Yankee teammates.

When the game started, there were cheers as the Orioles took the field. Mimi was not in the starting lineup, but the manager told him to be ready. He would be entering the game in the fifth or sixth inning. After the national anthem, Mimi returned to the Yankee dugout and could not help but reflect on the journey that brought him here today. He risked his life in his first escape attempt only to wind up back in Cuba facing harassment. There was the grueling time spent away from baseball, the depression that at times almost convinced him that his dream had turned to ashes. His palms were sweating as he sat in the dugout.

In the top of the sixth inning, Mimi was called upon to pinch hit. He walked slowly toward the batter's box. This was his first official at-bat in a Yankee game wearing the pinstripes. He was finally in the uniform he always dreamed of wearing. It didn't matter that it was only spring training. As he circled around the catcher, his heart was beating fast. He took a deep breath and dug in his spikes. The pitcher's name was Hank O'Leary. Mimi took Willie's advice. He had been watching the pitcher closely and played the at-bat out in his head. *I'm getting a first pitch fast ball. He hasn't been able to get his breaking stuff over the plate. He thinks as a pinch hitter I am going to take the first pitch.*

Mimi was right. The fast ball came. Mimi swung and smashed the ball to deep center field. Fans cheered as the ball sailed over the wall. As Mimi rounded first base, he thought of his dad. Between second and third base, he felt his heart pounding through his chest as he took a deep breath and smiled. When he approached home plate, he saw Manny, Anna, and Willie standing as they cheered.

THE END

POSTSCRIPT

In recent years all star caliber Cuban baseball players such as Yasiel Puig, Jose Abreu, Yoenes Cespedes, and Aroldis Chapman have defected to the United States and are leaving their mark on major league baseball. The amount of money at stake has increased dramatically. As a result, more elaborate and dangerous smuggling operations have evolved.

In 2014 President Obama made it part of his agenda to overhaul United States policy toward Cuba. His visit to Cuba in March of 2016, which included attending a baseball game between Tampa Bay Rays and the Cuban National Team, was the first by a sitting president in nearly ninety years. While the lifting of economic sanctions reinforced in the Helms-Burton Act of 1996 would require congressional action, the Obama administration took steps to reestablish diplomatic relations (including the reopening of the American Embassy in Havana), ease travel restrictions, and provide expanded opportunities for the sale and export of goods and services from the United States to Cuba.

Major League Baseball would like to ensure that the Cuban players no longer encounter the dangers of a secret boat trip or risk kidnapping and exploitation by smugglers. There remains skepticism over whether the Cuban government will ever allow its players to freely come to the United States. Currently, Cuban players are allowed to go to Japan or South Korea, provided they return for the Cuban baseball season. And in those instances, the Cuban government retains control over the contracts and even receives a significant portion of the player's salary. Officials of the Obama administration and Major League Baseball met for the purpose of creating an entirely new system that would allow MLB to scout and sign players in Cuba. Once signed, the players and their families would receive visas to travel between two countries.

While the Trump administration has scaled back the ability of Americans to travel to or conduct business with Cuba, much of the current administration's policy leaves in place many of the measures introduced by President Obama. Embassies in both countries will remain open. Direct commercial flights and cruises from the U.S. will still operate. Travelers can spend unlimited amounts of money on the island. Americans can send money to Cubans. The "wet foot, dry foot" policy that Obama eliminated will not be reintroduced. The economic embargo, however, remains in place and it could only be modified by an act of Congress.

As United States-Cuba relations move into the future, there is no doubt that the game of baseball will play an important role affecting the future relations between the two countries.

Brian David is a semi-retired attorney living in Chicago with his wife Cookie. He received his undergraduate degree from the University of Wisconsin, Madison and law degree from the University of Illinois. For thirty years he specialized in the representation of professional baseball players.